Stream

Dark Souls

George R. Mead

E-Cat Worlds Press

This is a work of fiction. All the characters and events portrayed are creations of the imagination, nothing more, nothing less.
Comments and questions? –> gmead01@gmail.com

Stream.

Copyright 2017 by George R. Mead

LCCN 2017940443

Mead, George R.
Stream. Special Investigator. /
George R. Mead.
p. cm. – Stream. Dark Souls
ISBN-13 978-0-9890927-3-9
1. Fantasy. I. Title. II. Series.

E-Cat Worlds established its publishing program as a reaction to the large commercial publishing houses currently dominating the book industry and the smaller intellectual clones. It is interested in publishing works of fiction and non-fiction that are often deemed insufficiently profitable or commercial or that are not necessarily reflective of current literary trends and fads.

E-Cat Worlds, 57744 Foothill Road, La Grande OR 97850
www.ecatworldspress.com
SAN 255-6383

In the middle of nowhere - Creativity.

First Edition:
Printed in the United States of America

Fiction

From Grandeville.
Portal
Lair
Not Again
And Again.
Magiwitch
Rebirth
Offspring
Holiday
Treasure
E'Nilt
Braidna
Seemna and Chyndra

A Tale of The Feyra
Jonathon and Dee
Dee Of The Fontala
Dee and The People
Dee and The Golden Cartouche

The Seven Lands
Seventeen Siblings (assisted by Zakke L. Zacog)

Stream
Special Investigator.
Dark Souls.

Nonfiction

A History of Union County
The Ethnobotany of the California Indians, 2nd Edition
A History of The Chinese in The West: 1848-1880
Yachats. The Town Called "Dark Water at the Foot of the Mountains."

"You can't blame a writer for what the characters say."

Truman Capote

The Warrior That Could Not Die

Soooo . . . . .
    There he was . . . . .

There he was . . . . .
    Sprawling . . . .

There he was, sprawled on his back, legs pointing downhill, on top of just lots and lots and lots of rusty red rock and rusty red soil.

He wasn't resting.

Up there he could see the clear blue sky, somewhat blurred by the cloud of rusty red dust slowly drifting away.

Of course, he had seen that clear blue sky just a few moments before. Even longer ago than that, when they were walking along the trail. Without all that rusty red dust in the air.

He and Stream had worked a number of long weeks editing and assembling a number of reports and she had decided, in her usual fashion, that it was time for them to have some R'n'R, rest and relaxation. This decision meant that they were going camping, in the way out there.

Off they went, to a very quiet, very isolated place that was sitting on the edge of nowhere, in the way out there, as she described it. Here was a vast extent of dry rusty red soil, rusty red rocks, it was a very rusty red environment.

After setting up their camp in that edge of nowhere, in the way out there, camp spot, they had loafed, talked, played cribbage, and rested, a whole lot of rest, which was the idea for coming here.

On the third day they had decided, she had suggested, he had agreed, to take a very leisurely hike, just to get a little exercise.

She wore her usual light green boots, blue jeans, light blue shirt.

He wore dark brown hiking boots, loose dark brown many pocket trousers, and a light tan shirt.

Several hours into their hike, walking along a narrow trail that followed the edge of the tall, mostly vertical wall of a deep rusty red arroyo, it happened.

Oh boy, did it!

Happen!

Did it ever happen!

It was a surprise. It was a very big surprise, what happened.

As the trail was quite narrow for a stretch on this section of the trail they were walking along in single file, stopping now and then to admire the view.

And . . .

Then here he was . . .

Down here . . .

Really surprised . . .

For reasons only known to Mother Nature, a sizable piece of the cliff wall had decided that it was time to relocate downward.

For reasons only known to The Goddess of Chance, Lou had been at that moment standing on top of this errant piece of real estate when it had decided to relocate.

So now . . .

Here he was . . .

Down here . . .

Really surprised . . .

Sprawling on top of, more or less, many cubic yards of rusty red deposited to the bottom of the cliff, a piece of the vertical side wall. It had been a very large chunk. It had made a sizable mound. It had created a wide and deep dent in the rest of the vertical side wall.

And so, here he was, on top of it, the rubble. Much to his surprise.

Finally, after admiring the sky and rusty red dust cloud, he wiggled his fingers and then his toes and decided that it was not too bad, all things considered. As far as he could tell at the moment, all he had broken, or rather he had broken for him, was his left forearm.

Satisfied that his spinal column was still functional, he had run his right hand over the injured member and was pleased to feel a smooth surface not ruptured by a jagged bone sticking out here or there. Eventually, he would have to get an X-ray done to find out what was what. But here and now, he decided that it was most likely cracked rather than broken.

So, all in all, it was not too bad.

Behind him he heard a rattling and slithering noise.

Damn, more cliff coming to join him and its errant portion.

Something thumped just behind the top of his head.

Good, it missed.

A very pleasant voice with just a touch of purr, asked, "Hey there, Lou. How ya doing?"

"Stream?" His voice came out more rasp than voice.

"Yep." She walked carefully around him until he could

see her peering intently down at him, eyes carefully checking this and that.

She frowned. "Be O.K. if I help you sit up?"

"Sure. Already did a broken back check." This time his voice sounded sorta normal instead of a harsh rasp.

She bend and did. Help him sit up.

Then she used her bandana and a little water to clean his face, some of his face.

"Ummmmm, not much cleaner, but not so much dust, gives you a nice red skin tone, sorta Hollywood injun looking." She grinned at him. And winked. Her mother was a tribal member, from a very long lineage. She added, with a sly wink, "With clothes to match. You are sorta red all over."

"Thanks." He managed a crooked smile. Then unbuttoned his shirt and slowly eased his left forearm into the opening and then buttoned the shirt to make an emergency sling.

"Hafta ta do," he grumbled and spit out some dirt. The spit was the same color of everything else in their immediate environment.

"Were you trying to kill yourself?" He frowned sternly up at her. "Coming down that way."

She laughed. It was her usual happy laugh, mainly directed at his comment about injuring herself.

"Nope. Just the fastest way down. If I used the trail it would have been a couple of hours before I could get here, even hurrying. Figured that you could probably use a little help sooner rather than later. Think you can walk?"

She certainly hoped so. He was far too heavy for her to carry him very far. It was a long way back to their camp.

"Help me stand and we will see what sort of hobble I

have."

She did and watched him carefully make his way down the debris mound to the arroyo floor.

Standing, looking up, swaying from side to side, he watched her make her way down to join him and frowned at her.

She pointed, ignoring that frown. "Way down there we will come to a trail that we can take to get back to the top."

"I thought," it was now her turn to frown, "that you were a dead duck for sure, for sure."

"Nope." He smiled, it was a rather crooked smile. "Quack, quack."

"Come'on, duckie," she waved, and pointed. "Let's hobble that way. Want some water? To drink. We won't worry about any more clean until we get out of here."

"Sure."

She shrugged off her pack, yanked out a bottle, opened it, and handed it to him.

"Far as I could tell, your pack is somewhere under all that. Total loss. It is a surprise that you weren't somewhere under all that with it."

"Surprised me too." He shrugged. And took a small drink, and handed the bottle back to her. "Thanks." *He had no idea why he hadn't wound up buried under all that dirt along with his pack. He didn't remember unloading his pack on the way down. It must have just been a reflex.*

And on they walked. Well, she walked, he mostly staggered. It was a very wobbly gait.

Stream kept an eye on him, frowning.

His stagger seemed to be getting worse the further they

went, the wobble more extreme.

Finally, deciding he really was getting worse, she stopped. His lurch was getting extreme.

Time for some desperate measures if she was going to get him out of here, alive.

Shrugging off her pack, she opened it and began to rummage around, and took out a small metal box. Popping the latch, she opened it, took out what she wanted, closed it, latched it, and stuffed the box back in her pack. Straightening up, she uncapped a water bottle.

"Open your mouth, Lou."

He did.

She shoved the pills in and handed him the water bottle. "Take a big drink and swallow those babies."

He did and blinked at her. "Wha . . . ?"

She took back the bottle, placed it in her pack, And lifted the pack back onto her back.

"Pretty quick you are not going to feel any pain at all. It is the only thing that I can do to get you out of here."

"Sure." He nodded, and turned. "Let's go." *It sounded like a plan to him.*

On they trudged. But his stagger had lessened. Some.

Soon, Lou's mind began to wander, partially from the battering he had taken, partially from whatever Stream had made him swallow.

His body, however, was on auto-pilot, just lurching along next to her.

His mind drifted, he remembered high school and sports.

He had tried them all, each in their season, and found that baseball was boring, that he wasn't really interested in knocking people around, which ruled out football. He didn't like basketball.

But he liked to run, so track was it. In that sport he liked cross-county running. It was a solo activity, just him and the route that he had to follow. One day, as he was cruising along, he remembered a phrase that he heard somewhere, *The Loneliness of the Long Distance Runner,* and realized that it was true. But, to him this wasn't a sad thing, it was just a fact of being, not exactly boring to him. It was fun. And he didn't feel alone either.

Out of high school he joined the military. During training he found that he had an interesting ability. It was a surprise of a sort. He had a unique skill. If he held a weapon, he could hit whatever he aimed at. It was his eyes, his mind, and his reaction time, all working together without conscious thought.

With that skill, practiced and improved upon, he wound up in a very special unit, a unit with a select few personnel whose assignments engaged them in very dangerous events.

Over time many of this unit died in various ways. It was taken as a cost of doing what they did.

One of his team, the overall organization of the unit was made up of teams of two members, who survived the last engagement, told Lou towards the end of this career, "Dude, you are the warrior who could not die!"

This particular statement had come from his current team-mate as Lou and he were lying side by side in adjoining beds recovering from a particularly messy activity that they had been involved in. Lou's team-mate had received numerous injuries and was, at the moment, wrapped in yards and yards of bandages covering a rather large number of places.

Lou was under observation by the medical folk as all they could see on the outside were bruises and contusions. They thought he had to have internal injuries even though they couldn't find any. So, they kept him under observation, just in case.

Lou laughed at the strange comment and suggested to his team-mate, "Well, you are still alive."

His team-mate received an early discharge. Lou spent the rest of his time in the organization continuing to do the usual thing, more of the same. In the process he collected a number of additional scars from the usual happenings.

When he was discharged and became a civilian again, everything, physically and mentally, pretty much worked as well as it did before he had joined up. So, he figured it was all to the good.

He wandered from occupation to occupation, from college course work to university course work then elsewhere, learning all manner of things and gaining all manner of additional experience, some of which included hazardous activities. He survived, others didn't. Then he wound up in an agency that also felt they required his skill set now and then. It paid well.

Then, one day, he received an invitation from yet another outfit to come for a "job interview." This invitation was delivered by two polite but determined men, who took him for a ride to the place of the interview.

The entire interview had been comprised of Lou being told, by the boss of whatever organization it was, that he was being hired to work with only one other person and to make sure that this person was not harmed. This person was a unique and special person. Lou's, um, previous work experience meant that he was qualified for the job and therefore he was now hired. At a very nice salary doing mostly office work and whatever else his immediate boss required him to do. And that would be his only job and his only responsibility.

Lou nodded, went home to produce his qualification sheet for the job, And then, there he was, working in a very interesting organization with a very interesting person. Of course, as he found out, there was more to it than just office work.

"HEY!"

He jerked back into awareness and stared at her.

Stream grabbed him by the shoulders and pointed him in the correct direction.

"UP! We are going up this trail. The truck is up there. PAY ATTENTION! UP! UP! UP!"

He nodded and shambled up the game trail, Stream right behind, gently shoving him along.

Lou's mind drifted off again into memories of things exploding, of things on fire, of bodies flying and of bodies falling.

His eyes popped open.

Stream stood at the end of his bed, an obvious hospital bed.

"Welcome back, Lou." She smiled. "It has been a few days. They turned off the stuff that kept you under. The Doc says that you can leave tomorrow morning after he makes a few more checks on whatever he thinks he needs to make a few more checks on. As far as they can find, you have lots of bruising and abrasions. There is a cracked bone in your left forearm with a light weight thing on it to keep immobile, but it is not broken. So that is it." She laughed. "Not too bad for a guy that rode a big chunk of real estate to the bottom of that arroyo."

She pointed at the large flower collection in two containers next to the head of his bed.

"Rala, The Squirrel, sent those."

He nodded. "Tell her thanks."

"You can after I pick you up in the morning. I've had your clothes cleaned and, um, repaired. They're hanging in your closet."

She spun toward the door and waved one hand over her shoulder.

"See ya. Time to go to work."

She was out and down the hall.

He nodded to himself. *Well, I didn't die.*

Upstairs in the office of The Head of Medical Services, Dr. Jonas Frazen leaned back in his swivel chair and frowned at Dr. James Jimenson, called J. J. by one and all.

"It is true!" J. J. set the large folder of X-rays and the results from other medical devices on the desk top.

"From what we were told about the patients accident, I felt we ought to do a rather comprehensive review of his entire skeletal system, starting with his spinal cord."

He sighed. "From everything that we saw, this guy has been, um, let's say, battered a whole lot of times."

He smiled at Jonas.

"As you well know, any injury to the skeleton shows

up." He laughed. "The body may be self-repairing, but it doesn't return everything back to its original factory condition. This patient has had an amazing life prior to this most recent event."

J. J. reached out and patted the thick folder. "See for yourself." He shrugged. "Whatever he did in his past, I am amazed that he is still alive and in such good shape. He must have good genes."

He stood. "Well, I am off to sign his release. I see no reason to keep him. He is healthy with a stabilizing cast on one arm for a cracked bone. The company that he works for told intake to charge them for whatever we thought was necessary. No questions, no haggle. Just do it, we'll pay for it."

He opened the door. "Let's have lunch around one-o-clock."

Then he strolled down the hall, whistling happily. Life working in a hospital was interesting. At times.

A Pretty Good Idea

Ignatius Willum Ranpan was wandering the halls of the organization, the company he had recently renamed *ReVal* (Research & Evaluation), deep in thought. He did this every once in awhile.

However, when he met one of the staff, he stopped and talked with them about whatever project they were working on, their thoughts that they might have on how to make the organization better, or about nothing in particular. Everyone of the staff had unique abilities, which was why they had been selected and hired. Not one of them had ever quit to take a "better" job. High job satisfaction was a goal of the company. Of course, this was coupled with a very, very good salary.

He smiled slightly to himself as he wandered. This organization, his organization, was as unique as the people who worked for it.

He almost laughed out loud. If only all those characters he knew from high school could see it and understand. Of course, they would not be able to do that. It was a very private company. It wasn't open to casual visitors of any kind.

I.W. was known among the folk who helped him create the company, the movers, the shakers, the money crowd, as they were often called. He knew that they would be surprised if he told them to call him "Iggy I.Q.," that awful nickname thrown at him from grade school through high school. It was interesting having that happen to him as he was not the stereotypic Geek, just a very bright person.

After happily leaving high school behind, he had

collected a number of degrees from the colleges and universities that had course work in subjects and programs that he was interested in.

Then, one day, as he was walking down the street, on a whim, he had popped into the campaign office of a politician that he thought seemed to have a working brain, just to have a little chat.

And, as the saying goes, the rest was history.

I.W., as he preferred to be called, became an "Adviser," due to the given advice, the very useful advice that he had offered to that politician.

And the word spread.

Over time, he became very well known among those who had suggested to him, ever so carefully, that any help, any advice, he could offer them would be very, very appreciated.

So, he helped them, he advised them, but only to those who paid attention to that advice. Those who didn't, he would no longer talk to or with.

And the word spread.

Those he did talk to found that their careers tended to be in an upward direction.

I.W. was in demand.

But the demand on his decisions didn't have any effect as to he might decide to talk to, only honesty.

The end result was that the number of folk that he did talk to became a fairly small group, but a very successful small group.

I.W. enjoyed what he was doing.

It was fun.

For him.

It was a fateful day, at least that was how he saw it, when he had a rather casual conversation with a member of one of the large agencies who were involved in legal affairs keeping illegal affairs under control. He had heard a comment in their wandering conversation that he had heard before. So he did what he always did when his curiosity was aroused.

He visited, he talked, he gathered information.

When he was done, when he had formulated a solution to the problem that he saw, he had a gathering of a number of people that he felt ought to be interested in what he would propose.

To him, the concept was simple. There ought to be a special organization, a special company, one that would be very private, very, very private.

The function of that company would be to do what was not being done.

It would be a research and evaluation company, research of a very special kind. The results of this company's research and evaluation activity would be given, as final and detailed reports, to the appropriate agencies to act upon that information in the best way that they saw fit, given the problem being addressed in those reports, with all claims for credit going to the agency involved.

The basic premise of the company was that the legal authorities at all levels usually did not have the resources to truly do a complete and very, very thorough job of investigation on the problems that they were handed. This was usually due, in the main, from a lack of resources, economic resources, a lack of manpower to be allowed to only work on that problem, and the goals and activities of whatever agency it was that were being twisted and misguided by the often self-centered mindset of various politicians.

I.W. stated that this new company would be immune, free of these impediments, as it would be a very private and independently funded organization, thoroughly legal in all aspects of its known operation. But it would not be political, nor would it allow itself to become mired in any political nonsense of any kind.

The company would do research on any problem that the various legal agencies might submit to it, with one caveat, of all the problems suggested, the company would only select from four to six to work on at a time. The company staff would work on the problem starting with the materials submitted for as long as it took to reach an end point prior to releasing a final report. They would use whatever additional research methods they felt were appropriate. Once that final report, or reports, were delivered, his company would never be identified in any manner whatsoever as the place from which that report came. Any breach of this by the agency receiving the report would forever put that agency outside the pale as far as the company was concerned. And no manner of waving the flag or anything else would change that.

I.W., as the head of the company, would have sole authority as to which four to six "problems" would be worked on.

He had handed to each of his selected group a single sheet of paper listing exactly how the recipient of that single sheet of paper could help. If they couldn't do these things then the creation of such a company would be a no-go. There would be no compromise, no watering down of the concept. If, after the company came into existence, an attempt by any agency to successfully stick their nose into its behavior, would cause an immediate dissolution of the company. It would dissolve like snow in a rain storm. And everyone else would lose.

Within a week he had all the resources, economic, political, legal, he had asked for. He began to build.

It was a very slow and careful process as he had very specific types of folk in mind. These folk were hard to find. He sent out feelers through his personal network, the one he had built over a long period of time.

And the word spread.

Little by little, he met and interviewed the selected folk.

He hired those that fit.

He spend much time and effort selecting the building to house the company. Then he spent more time and money altering it to fit the company requirements for the safety and the research needs of its staff as well as their personal safety elsewhere, that is, when they were not only "in-house."

The company began to accept "projects" and over time it became apparent to the agencies that those final reports were doing exactly what I.W. had said they would do. The final results greatly exceeded the expectations of the recipients.

So, he wandered the halls of the company deep in thought and pondered what else, if anything, needed doing.

To Seek, To Find

He was wandering.

Not really. He was walking. He had a purpose.

He was walking through an area that had no roads, ancient or modern. There were no trails although there were a few small indications that some animals had infrequently passed through this dry, rocky, sandy, open space.

The vegetation, what there was of it, was infrequent and widely dispersed.

Aerial photographs hadn't shown anything else.

But.

He was walking.

For some time he had been walking. He had set out, a considerable distance from where he currently was walking.

As the sun had set he sat and listened to the silence, and sang soft song.

And waited.

The next day, he stood.

And started walking.

He was walking.

He was headed in the direction that felt right.

He had told the others when they had last gathered that he was going to do this thing.

Far to the north of where he was walking The Ancient Ones had build great structures.

Then he had sat again and sang soft song and listened to the silence.

Now he was walking.

In an arrow straight line.

His eyes watched carefully.

All the maps, all the current knowledge, all the photographs indicated that here, in this emptiness, there was nothing.

He walked.

His eyes watched carefully.

He stopped.

It was late in the day.

The sun was setting beyond the far horizon behind him, casting long shadows from imperfections in the ground, from small and large rocks, from the infrequent vegetation.

He saw it.

He saw an edge. He saw the tiny exposed edge of a carved stone block, just visible next to a small clump of vegetation.

He smiled, walked over, and sat next to it and carefully examined the space around him.

He sat for two days.

He carefully searched the environment.

He listened to the emptiness.

Then he stood and strolled away.

To tell the others

At their gathering, he handed around an aerial photograph with a small mark on it.

Then they planned how they would do what was required, how to do it in such a manner that none of their activities nor what he had found would leave a visible mark.

A year passed as they planned and gathered the necessary materials.

Four years passed of very careful work, careful work that was always aware of modern devices looking down from the sky.

They were determined.
They were careful.
They were successful.

Now they were gathered on a dark, moonless night, all of them.

For four years they had worked. They worked when the moon was dark. They worked when storms blew unimpeded across the open desert reaches. They worked as the winds blew away all signs of their activities.

Slowly, carefully, they worked.

They worked so curious eyes peeking from above would not see what they were doing at this place. They left nothing to draw the attention of a curious eye.

They worked to empty the structure of everything that had filled it and hidden it from view. They believed, they knew, that those hundreds of years of storms and winds had done this so they could find it and reclaim it.

Now they were here, on a dark moonless night, every one of them.

They sat in two rows, facing each other, sitting on the hard packed dirt floor of the tall cylinder of carefully constructed stone.

At one end of the double line, a small fire of very dry wood burned in the round fire pit.

At the other end of the double line there was a small hole in the floor, the sign of all that they believed and knew to be their true history.

Each of the men wore loose capes draped over their shoulders that were made from the pelts of coyote, owl, fox, or crow, signifying the one that had come to them in their early years.

Now having their own place, their own place of mystery and power, they had somewhere to keep their things, the things that friends and neighbors could not accidently find, accidently stumble over, and bring to their owner a slow death.

For the first time ever, they felt safe in their knowledge, the knowledge they had worked so hard to acquire, here in the spell of the swelling power that was to come.

This night, for the first time, they were all gathered together, singing the songs as several of their members drew the painting on the floor between the two rows, thumb and forefinger slowly releasing the thin stream of ash to create the painting, the painting that reinforced the power of the songs that they sang.

Here they sat, bodies decorated with paint, wearing masks and jewelry, feeling the power of their animal souls.

The sing would take most of the night.

Before sunrise they would leave and scatter, careful to leave no trace. They would scatter, back to their homes and their lives, just one among the many.

Each would carefully plan and execute their part in that which must be done. And it would be done, the true effect hidden.

Another Day, Another . . .

Stream knocked on the door and pushed it open.

Well, he certainly looks healthy in spite of falling off a cliff along with a large piece of it.

"Heya, Lou, ready to go? Signed out?"

Lou stood and nodded.

"Yep."

Stream smiled.

"I parked right in front."

She spun, walked from the room and waited for him in the hall. They walked to the elevator and eventually exited the main entrance to the hospital.

Her large pickup, dusty and unwashed as usual, sat in one of the short-time visitor slots.

They climbed in.

She started the truck and headed them down the street.

Lou twisted around in his seat and looked out the rear window.

"Where are we going? The office is back that way."

She laughed, her usual very happy laugh.

"The boss said to go this way."

"Oh?"

Lou leaned back and watched the traffic and waited for an explanation.

Now what? This was certainly not being done like anything else that they had done before. Other than her dragging him to a new place to have a meal. Or to another camping spot.

Four blocks down the street, three blocks to the right, six

blocks to the left, Stream parked them in front of a store.

Lou looked out the side window.

The store sign, ornate red letters outlined with bright green borders stated that it was *Pack'In*.

Stream opened her door, jumped down and waved him to come along.

As he followed her inside, she explained, "The boss said to buy you new gear as most of your's is somewhere under a very large amount of rusty red dirt and rock."

She pointed down one of the aisles.

"Most of the ultra-light backpacking gear is that way. Select whatever you like, just pile it all on the checkout counter. Take your time. I have a few things that I want to look at." She shrugged. "As long as we are here."

She beamed at him. "Ahhhhh, don't worry about the cost, O.K.? When the boss said to do this he was quite firm about that. He gave me a credit card."

She headed off in another direction as Lou wandered down the aisle she had indicated.

Everywhere that Lou looked he saw folk who obviously liked being outdoors a lot, a whole lot. Faces and hands had that brownish look you only see from the folk who do. For the most of them he saw no extra weight being carried on their bodies. It was just a bunch of very healthy folk wandering around in a store that supplied them with the proper gear they required to look like that.

An hour later, more or less, Stream strolled toward the checkout counter, a new sleeping bag tucked under one arm, her free hand holding a new, very small, very light, ultra-efficient stove.

Lou was waiting, patient as ever, beside a sizable pile of

gear heaped in a cart.

Stream stopped and laughed.

"Looks like you are ready?"

Lou nodded. He had watched her approach.

She doesn't appear to be aware of how she really affects the people around her with that happy laugh. Her jet black hair made those blue eyes seem to sparkle an even brighter blue when she did.

"Yep," he said. "Ready."

Stream dumped her stuff on the checkout counter.

"Just pile it all here," she said to him as she handed the credit card to the young man standing behind the counter. "It all goes on this card," she told him.

The clerk nodded and tried not to stare at her. He quickly began to run everything from the large mound of gear before him into the register.

Then he shoved a long slip that the register had hiccuped to her. She spun it around and signed it, without checking, took back the credit card and stuffed it into a shirt pocket.

The pair guided the heaped cart out to her truck and set all their purchases in the back of the truck. The rear seat held the flowers from his hospital room. Lou returned the cart to its parking place, walked back, and clambered into the truck.

As she drove from the parking lot and then down the street, she took a quick glance at him, his soft grey eyes looked back, then she focused on the traffic in front of them.

"What?" asked Lou.

"The boss thinks that you are a pip!"

"Huh?"

"Pretty important person."

"Oh?"

He shrugged. And looked at her.

The real pip was driving, not sitting on the passenger side.

When he was hired the boss told him that being her Assistant had been predicated upon his abilities as expressed from many of his past activities. Lou hadn't commented, but he had been surprised. Most of that stuff was supposed to be buried deep in files that no-one was supposed to be able to access. That told him that there was much more to being an Assistant in this company than he was being told. And ever much more, as he had found out.

"Pip, pip, old chap!" She laughed, a happy laugh at her joke.

"Sure," he said.

As she swung her rig around a corner, he leaned forward and stared out the windshield.

"Wrong way! My place is in the other direction."

"Nope, not today. We are going to my place. You can have the large bedroom at the end of the hall, umm, for a few days."

"Ah?"

"Think of it as a health watch. That was quite a fall you took, you and all that cliff face."

"Oh. Sure. You cooking?"

"Unless you have talents so far kept hidden, I am."

"Some."

"Which one? Breakfast or dinner?"

"Uh, breakfast."

"I am an early riser, partner."

"No problemo."

"O.K., Arnold." She winked at him.

She parked in her parking area, closed the outside gate, and helped him with the carrying of their purchases into the house. Standing in the hall, she pointed.

"We will store all that stuff in that room, food in the kitchen."

After they had put everything away, she walked back to the living room, and then returned to the kitchen, carrying a large basket of flowers that was bedecked with ribbons and bows that had been sitting on one of the living room small tables. In the center of the flowers a large bottle stuck up.

He looked at it as she set it on one side of the kitchen table next to the flowers from Lou's hospital room.

"Co . . . han," she said, yanking the bottle free to check the label. Somehow, in spite of the locked gate, he had managed to deliver it.

Lou winced. "I am not going to drink any of that stuff."

"It is just a very good red wine, not his usual brew." She put it back.

"Oh."

Cohan's brew was made from a recipe that was noted for its ability to make the one who imbibed it rather numb after a few sips. He remembered the one time he and Stream had drunk some of Cohan's last present.

She smiled at him.

"The dark blue towels are your's, the bright yellow ones are mine."

He nodded.

Obviously this had been planned ahead of time.

"We going in?" And looked the question at her.

"Nope. Things are rather quiet. Nothing to be in a big rush about. Just a few small reports that we need to put together."

"Sure."

"Feel like taking a stroll around the neighborhood?"

"Sure."

They did.

They wandered around and through the surrounding

blocks, stopping now and then to look at something she pointed out, to talk with this person or that person, all of whom evidently knew Stream quite well and seemed to recognize him from past perambulations the pair had made around the neighborhood.

Many blocks and turns later, she halted at a small trailer and ordered tacos from the serving window. They sat at one of the small folding tables, under the portable awning, and ate their purchases.

By the time they returned and were seated at the kitchen table, it was late afternoon.

She made coffee. They sat and sipped the very dark brew and munched on cookies. She had bought a bag of them, a small brown paper bag of homemade cookies, from someone's grandmother.

As they sat and sipped and munched, the front door banged open.

Rala, nicknamed "The Squirrel," hurried into the kitchen. Her nickname came from her job as an analyst, one who had the ability to "squirrel around" in raw data and see patterns most folk completely missed. She also had the keys to Stream's house and gate.

She was carrying a large cast iron kettle by its wire handle, the top covered with a clear glass lid.

"It is dinner," she announced proudly as she set it on the stove. "I made it! Lamb stew. I combined four recipes that I found on the internet."

She poured a cup of coffee, took a few cookies, and then explained, in detail, exactly what she had done.

Glancing at the kitchen clock, she jumped up and set the burner under her kettle to a very low flame.

"It needs to simmer for two more hours."

She beamed at them.

"The boss told me to take the day off and that you would be at home. Soooooooooo, here I am."

She plopped into the chair next to Lou and pulled her coffee cup over.

"Thanks for the flowers," he said. "They were really nice."

She nodded, a very shy nod.

Lou smiled at her. "Stream told me. There was no card." He pushed the cookie bag over to her.

"Cookie?"

Rala looked in the bag, and took two more.

After taking a bite, she said, "The boss has been prowling the halls again."

Lou looked at Stream.

"He does that every once in awhile," she explained. "He is just thinking about the company and the staff and if there is something he ought to do to make things better."

"Oh." Lou filled her cup, then his.

Rala stared at the large basket of flowers with the bottle sticking up in the middle.

"Strange arrangement."

"Cohan," explained Stream

"GOSH!" Rala's eyes flew wide. "You are not going to drink that, are you?"

"It is just a bottle of red wine. We can have it with dinner. I'll make a bunch of biscuits to go along with the stew. And a salad of course."

Long past dinner, the three sat in the living room talking about nothing of importance.

Rala told them, in detail, about a movie, a DVD, that she

had watched on her home computer, several times. She had a large display.

As Rala was winding up her discussion, Stream looked toward the front door and frowned, a very tiny frown.

Lou noticed, he always noticed, and slipped his hand into the jacket he had put on for dinner. Anything unwanted that came through that door was going to receive a number of small holes and might live, if lucky.

Stream looked at him and gave an almost imperceptible shake of her head.

He relaxed and took his hand out of his pocket.

Rala looked at her watch and stood.

"Time for me to go." She maintained a fairly rigid schedule.

Stream smiled at her. "I'll clean everything."

"Oh! Good!" Rala nodded vigorously. "Just bring the kettle to your office. I can get it there."

She headed for the door and stopped with her hand on the door knob. She looked back at Stream.

"Did you get a dog? There is one scratching at the door and wagging its tail."

Stream laughed.

Lou jerked.

That wasn't a happy laugh. That was a laugh of surprise. Sorta.

Rala nodded and opened the door.

The dog strolled in, took a quick sniff at Rala's pant leg, and headed for Stream. Lou watched it, carefully.

"Her name," said Stream, "is Moon Shadow. Ahhhh, a new acquisition."

Rala smiled at her. "Night." She hurried out, gently closing the living room door behind her. She had left the small door in the gate ajar but closed it on her way out.

Lou sat up.

"When did you get a dog?"

The dog sniffed Lou and sat next to Stream, looking up into her face.

"Just now, Lou, just now."

Problem

Round Tom Anders stood looking out his office window.

It was a small office with the usual clutter one would expect to find in such an office.

One, old, somewhat battered, wooden desk, an in/out basket perched on one corner of the desk, at the moment empty of documents, with an equally old and battered wooden swivel chair, which stood between him and the desk. There were three wooden chairs with round, somewhat comfortable, backs, sitting here and there. Against one wall stood three, four-drawer filing cabinets next to a small table, also against the wall, a coffee maker on top of the table, plunged into a handy outlet.

Round Tom had lived with his nickname since the seventh grade when his present physical shape had begun to appear. He was a rather round person with a light tan skin and dark hair. As his friends and fellow students had realized as soon as they entered High School, "Round" was not fat. It was all muscle. It ran in the male side of his family. When he began to play football it became apparent.

Round Tom, as he was known by everyone in this small, very rural, very isolated village, looked out his window at the plaza that was the central space and social center of the village. Today, as on most comfortable days, in terms of the local weather, the two places selling food, and the two places selling hard and soft beverages of all flavors, had set out tables and chairs for clients and just casual visitors, of which there very few.

He sighed. Two weeks ago the plaza had been swarming with folk, venders and booths selling food and all manner of things. It had been the usual celebration of the village's founding.

And, as it always did, it started Friday night, ran all day Saturday, way into the night, with cleaning and general restoration of the plaza happening on Sunday morning.

The celebration had been its usual orderly disorder. There had been a few fist fights and a few really drunk individuals. These had been the usual and well known folk, as much a part of the social fabric as the celebration. No one bothered to get very excited about either activity, mostly just nodding and telling each other that what can you do, it is just old so-and-so as usual, up to no good again.

Round Tom was the local law, generally called "Sheriff" by one and all. He had two deputies, both part time who mostly earned their living doing other things.

The village was small, the village budget was small, which explained that.

Round Tom was the only full time law, such as it was, mainly employed more as a social activity than law enforcement. He generally helped folk see that whatever they were doing to cause a problem had a better way of being resolved.

Behind him, the door banged open and bounced off the wall as someone stomped into his office, bellowing in their sometimes loud and harsh voice, "WHAT ARE YOU GOING TO DO ABOUT IT?"

He sighed again and slowly turned around.

Maize Elanor Hard glared at him.

It spite of the voice she was quite petite and not to hard on the eyes, in spite of her manner. Her eyes, dark as midnight, glared at him from under the mass of equally black hair framing her face.

"Hard," he mumbled in her general direction, using the name most folk addressed her with.

She had come by that label from marrying Alfred Hard, the owner of the only newspaper, such as it was, in the village. Alfred had died some time ago leaving all his wordily possessions to his wife who now was the sole proprietor and editor of the newspaper.

"Well?" she growled, moderating her voice to a low rumble.

"Not much," he said in response to *it* as he shrugged, "that I can do."

He waved one arm and spoke in her general direction, "We have searched five miles all around the village and we have found nothing, nothing at all. None of his friends and acquaintances, nor his folks, know anything useful either." He shrugged again.

"Soooooo, at the moment, it is a mystery," he stated firmly.

He spun his wooden swivel back around and dropped into it, propping his arms on the desk top.

"That is it, Maize," he stated, once again. They had this conversation again and again. "We sent everything we knew to the state folks so they can keep on the outlook for James. But that is all we can do. We don't know anything and we can't find out anything, that matters."

He nodded, mostly to himself and looked up at her.

"All we really know is that he, like most of the inhabitants hereabouts, was here Friday evening during the celebration. He was seen, here and there, early in the day on Saturday. After that no-one recalls seeing him anywhere."

He waved one hand vaguely at the plaza.

"Lots of outsiders at the celebration, as usual. Lots of folk, as usual, that we don't really know. Such a thing hasn't happened before. He never got into trouble, like some of his buddies did, and do."

He leaned back, the springs in the chair making their usual complaint.

"You will just have to write about something else. If we ever find out anything new, I will let you know."

Maize grumbled at him, spun round, and stomped her way from the room, slamming the still open door closed, firmly and loudly behind her.

Round Tom sighed, and tried to think of anything else that he could do.

Again

They parked in the same spot.

They established their camp in the same spot.

Early the next morning they set out on the same narrow trail.

The area they were camping and hiking in was all varying shades of red rust.

They were each carrying a small backpack packed with water, snacks, and lunch.

They headed out, Stream in the lead. The trail wandered along close to the edge of the deep arroyo.

She had decided that they ought to finish the trip that they had started a number of days in the past.

A few hours later they stopped.

Stream shrugged off her backpack and fished out her camera.

Just past where she stopped the trail ended, in a manner of speaking.

It ended at a large, jagged, sorta semi-circular break where the arroyo wall had fallen away.

On the other side of the gap they could see the trail wandering along the edge of the arroyo.

She smiled at him, walked over to the slide and began to take pictures of it. Finally satisfied, she walked back and stuffed her camera back into the pack and slipped the pack back in place on her back.

She smiled at Lou.

"Just thought that we ought to have some visual record

of where you took your ride."

Lou walked over and joined her in peering at the mound of what had once been the wall of the arroyo now lying on the arroyo floor.

He nodded.

"Pretty amazing all right."

It wasn't anything that he wanted to ever do again.

The walked around the edge of the collapsed section and rejoined the trail headed toward the foothills.

As they always did, they stopped here and there to look at this or that. It was a casual hike. It was a no-hurry hike.

In all directions it was a land of orange and rusty red tones. Here and there was small scatter of vegetation hardy enough to survive in a very low moisture environment.

Two hours later, following the narrow trail along the edge of the arroyo, they arrived.

At the ruins.

Stream shrugged off her backpack, leaned it against a stacked rock wall, fished out her lunch and sat down, and leaned against that same wall. She patted the open ground next to her side.

"Have a seat." She laughed softly.

He did after shedding his back pack and digging out his lunch.

He took a big bite from his sandwich and chewed slowly.

Stream wagged her sandwich at their surroundings and in two bites finished it.

"This is where we had been headed before you took that little detour along with a sizable chunk of the arroyo wall. I had thought that we could camp here for a few days. But." She sighed. "Not on this trip." And shrugged. "Next time."

"Ummm," he mumbled around his lunch.

"Right!" She yanked another sandwich from her backpack and began to eat it.

He nodded and once again wondered about her metabolic system.

"Where's your dog?" he asked after he swallowed a section of his sandwich.

"Moon Shadow?"

"Yep."

"She is off visiting her family."

"Huh?"

She grinned at him.

"She is not a dog."

"Oh?" He took another large bite. And chewed slowly.

"She is a Mexican Wolf. They are, or were, almost extinct hereabouts. But they are making a slow recovery aided by folk who believe that they ought to be running about in their original territory. You remember the Grey Wolves."

He nodded.

He remembered Stream's mother telling how a unique skill was passed through their female line in her tribe. It was an ability to speak with, to interact with, to know what a species of animal was thinking. That species recognized the person that could do that.

"In our peoples culture, at times, there are those that have abilities that allow them to see, or do, what most cannot. We do not worry about that, and we do not ostracize them. We just understand."

She waggled one hand toward the road entering the meadow from the forest that surrounded the place where she and her husband lived. "All those other folk out there do not understand. They always talk of superstition, or conjuring tricks."

"My mother's mother was a Special Child. My mother was not. I am. In terms of this modern world, there must have been some type *of genetic mutation long, long ago for new abilities that could passed on. I do not know of anyone who would do the proper research to truly know that. Suffice it to say that it does occur and one must accept whatever one is. From what my mother's mother told, it passes along the female line. But it does seems to skip generations in an unpredictable pattern. And as she told me, as she self-discovered, this ability is expressed when that female reaches a certain age."*

She laughed softly. *"Happy birthday, Stream daughter."*

He remembered walking the trails in the forest that surrounded her folk's place and meeting the wolf packs that lived in the region.

He remembered Stream sitting and talking with them, scratching behind the ears of one of the alpha males, a 150 pound monster.

Her ability, some strange genetic thing that no-one understood, happened to be with the wolves. As he was given to understand it, someone else might know hawks, or whatever.

Later, much later, he traveled with Stream as she hunted the three men that had been trying to kill her, her parents, and destroy the organization that he and Stream worked for. Mainly because those three men, the tri-part head of their vast criminal organization, had felt threatened by her.

They had walked along a jeep trail to the houses where they lived and killed them, aided by the local wolf pack in that isolated mountainous region.

He nodded and smiled at her.

Those guys had been way overdue.

"Yep. I remember the Grey Wolves."

She finished her sandwich and fished another from her pack.

"I have been thinking," she said around her first bite.

"About?"

"What we do."

"Umm."

"We read what is sent to us, if necessary we gather additional data and analyze it. We do that and double check, triple check it. Finally we write a report with all the supporting documentation and deliver it to the appropriate organization. We have no time pressure, we have no political pressure, we have no economic pressure, none of the things designed to bend our understanding or the final conclusions."

"Yep."

"But unlike most of the folk out there," she waggled the hand holding another of her sandwiches in a broad sweep, "we don't use any system of mythological thinking to effect our conclusions."

"Sure."

He wondered where she was going with this.

"Everywhere in the world people believe in things that are not so."

"Uh huh." Lou shrugged. Waiting.

"So, their belief bias their ability to think rationally. Look at my mother's culture. They, like everyone else, have a complex system of belief that says this is who we are and this is how the world came to be. None of it is true. It is just something that folk in the very long ago made up to satisfy themselves that it was a sufficient answer to questions that required grander answers to questions like, how did the world come to be the way it is, why are we here, where did we come from? Things like that. Now, because all these so-called answers have a great antiquity they are given a weight that they do not deserve. Even the astrophysicists engage in this sort of thing. None of them try to answer what was there before their big-bang. Did everything come from nothing? That is a mystical religious problem, not a rational one."

She sighed. "Look at me. I am kinna wolf, in a manner of speaking. But most of mother's culture gives it a sorta-religious meaning, not merely some strange ability that is inherited, which means genetic not mystic."

Stream took a big bite and chewed vigorously.

"I am tired of folk who want to believe in the equivalent of Snow White and The Seven Dwarfs trying to force me to accept their fairy tales."

"Ahhhhh?"

"What?"

"Does all this, um, dissertation have anything to do with what we are working on?"

She shook her head.

"Nope!"

"O.K."

"Just a grumble about the world."

Then she waved her free hand at their surroundings.

"Walllll, partner, I kinna figured to camp hereabouts a few days before you took your ride with that there cliff."

She spoke with the John Wayne drawl perfectly.

"But, pilgrim, as we got us a leetle backlog of work to do at work, so all we get is a single day to be out here enjoying the big open and then it is back to work."

He nodded.

"Sure."

He winked at her. "No problemo," replied Arnold.

She laughed, eyes sparkling.

Sorta Dumb

The phone rang at 2:00 a.m.

No one phoned at 2:00 a.m.

Not in this small community.

This place was about two dozen houses, more or less. It really depended upon what folk decided to call a house.

The people here abouts had been living here for generations. It was occupied by a population that was comprised of physically large folk, most over six feet tall, most were rather thick, from front to back and from side to side. Most of them, but not all.

It was mostly due to genetics.

Very hardy individuals had migrated into this area and for reasons never passed down as part of the local knowledge/folklore, had gotten along with the local tribal folk and had intermarried with them. The local natives, the indigenous folk, were mostly large folk as had been most of the early settlers/immigrants. Hence the physical shape of the present local population.

Nowadays, the few strangers that came down the track locally called a road, couldn't tell one group from the other, locals from natives. The locals and the natives could. But it was a very subtle thing.

Here and there, children were born with startling blue eyes, genetics at work.

The phone rang at 2:00 a.m.

He lurched up, rolled from the bed, and lumbered from the bedroom toward the living room via the kitchen.

The phone rang. Again.

It was 2:00 a.m. This was told to him by his alarm clock, glaring red numerals in the darkness of the kitchen, where the clock lived on the counter next to the coffee maker.

Rona, pronounced locally as Ro Nah, not Ron Ah as the few strangers who read his bronze name tag said his name.

Rona MacKenzie, lurched into the living room and yanked up the phone in a strangle hold. Far back in the dim distant past a large Scotsman had arrived, survived the encounter with the local tribe, and had taken a wife.

"Uh?" he grumbled into the phone.

Rona always answered the phone that way so whoever called wasn't put off by his response, not at all. The time of day had nothing to with his response.

He listened to the very excited voice and waited patiently for it to wind down before attempting a reply. Which he finally got to do.

"Ten minutes, well, maybe, twenty minutes."

He turned on the coffee maker. It was always loaded before he retired for the night.

By the time that the coffee maker was making its last steamy gasps, Rona had showered, dressed, and ran a brush through his thick black hair.

The brass name plate over his left pocket told all who looked that this person was "Officer Rona MacKenzie." His thick leather belt supported a very large holster and large revolver. It kinna reinforced the name plate statement.

A number of the locals used to ask him why he bothered with the name plate as they all knew who he was anyway. Others sometimes asked why he carried that large revolver instead of one of those nifty guns they saw in the few movies or television programs when they visited those few relatives that actually lived where one could see movies or watch television.

Rona pointed out to them that the reason he carried the gun he did is because that is the one he owned and practiced with every day. After all, in all the years he did what he was doing, he had never had to shoot anyone. So why would he need to spend a lot of money for a new and fancier weapon.

The name plate was because he thought that he ought to do that, have one. It was part of the job.

Standing next to the counter he made and packed four sandwiches, filled his thermos, turned off everything that needed turning off, and headed out of the kitchen into the normal night darkness of this region.

Climbing into his large and never to be washed truck, he headed for town, as everyone called this small cluster of houses, and aimed for the one where Slim Jem Halaban lived.

From his place, one of the few sorta isolated places, to her place was about a ten minute drive if one drove at the usual rate of speed around here, not too fast, not too slow. Slim Jem claimed a long distance ancestor had created the family name after some sort of argument with a relative.

As he approached town it appeared that every light in her place was on. Half a dozen trucks were parked close by in the usual haphazard disorder.

He parked, climbed down, carrying his sandwiches and coffee, walked up to the front door and rang the door bell. Usually he just knocked a couple of times and walked in. This time he thought he ought to be formal.

The door swung in and the brothers Charles and John waved him in, closed it behind him, and then stood in front of the closed door.

A number of men, and a few women, stood around the edges of the living room, blocking every window and doorway.

Slim Jem stood, next to the kitchen doorway, across the room facing the couch, shotgun pointing at the small man sitting by himself in the middle of that couch. Her finger was on the trigger.

From what Rona could see it appeared that the small man had been knocked around a bit before he wound up sitting on the couch.

Rona fetched a chair from the kitchen, leaving his sandwiches and coffee on the small table near the outside door, and sat down facing the couch, to one side of the line of fire of Slim Jem. She winked at him as he passed by and gave him a worried smile and a brief nod of her head.

"Uh," began Rona as he sat down, "someone want to explain."

Whoever this small man was, he wasn't from anywhere around here.

Charlie Chews A Lot, Rona's sorta part-time deputy cleared this throat and nodded.

"Him there tried to kidnap Johnny One Shoes young son who's screams emptied every house in town. Frank, Chester, Harold, and May Ann stopped him."

Rona nodded. Any one of them outweighed this guy by a hundred pounds or more as well being as at least a foot taller. It certainly explained how he came to look the way he did.

"Old Snap," continued Charlie, "wanted to shoot him then and there but I, eh ah, convinced him to, eh ah, wait."

Rona nodded. Old Snap stood in a far corner holding a hunting rifle, glowering at the guy on the couch.

Rona looked at their prisoner, carefully this time. Sorta old, unafraid, dressed somewhat peculiar. He wore a strange necklace and cape that looked to have been a coyote a long time ago.

"He say anything?" Rona asked all those standing around the room.

"Nope," stated Charlie. "Not a word. To anyone."

Rona nodded.

"You have a name, old man?"

Not a twitch.

Rona sighed, softly. "Why were you trying to take one of our children?"

Not a blink.

"You on drugs of any kind?"

Nothing.

Rona sighed, loudly this time. He looked around the room and back again.

"Anyone recognize which tribe this guy is from?"

The small man's eyebrows twitched upward.

Well that got a small reaction from him.

Rona looked over at Wide Annie, otherwise known as Mary Ann, who looked to be ready to loose control and do bad things to this guy.

"Annie, could you go over and speak to Charity Jane and ask her and her grandmother to come over here? I am sure that Slim Jem will cook up some beer pancakes for them."

That would probably do the trick to get them to come over.

"Ump," replied Wide Annie as she headed out the front door on the errand.

Slim Jem headed into her kitchen and began to make breakfast for everyone.

Rona stood, walked into the kitchen, and back again, carrying a stack of heavy duty thick white plates and a fistful of knives and forks.

He gave one of each of everything to everyone except that guy on the couch. At the moment Rona was not inclined to do anything for him until he knew more about what had been going on. Not at all inclined.

As various mouth watering odors drifted from the kitchen into the living room, smiles of various sizes and shapes began to appear on folk's faces.

Slim Jem was well know for her culinary skills, and one or another of everyone in the room, at various times, had been treated to one of her breakfasts.

But one and all kept their eyes fastened on that guy on the couch.

Any sudden movement that he might make would certainly result in his being damaged by all those knives, forks, and dishes, if not the various firearms within handy reach. If such an event happened, all would see that Slim Jem would have suitable replacements for damaged or broken items, including the couch.

As everyone began consuming pancakes and bacon, the front door banged open and Wide Annie clumped in, rifle clenched in one hand.

She was followed in by Charity Jane and her grandmother.

The grandmother thumped into the house, a thick hiking stick keeping time on the floor with her steps.

THUMP!

THUMP!

THUMP!

Rona stood, handed each of them a plate, knife and fork, and pulled out a chair for the grandmother.

When Rona was a very young child she was there and was called grandmother. He had never heard anyone call her anything other than grandmother. There were as many tales as there were inhabitants of the town as to exactly how old grandmother was and what her given name was.

Rona collected the plates and hardware as each signaled that they were done. All eyes watched grandmother and that guy.

Grandmother slowly cut precise pieces from her pancakes and bacon strips. Then she slowly chewed each piece.

There were times when Rona was convinced that much of what she did was theater. He thought that now. But he knew better than say anything.

Grandmother finally shoved the plate in his direction.

He took everything back to the kitchen and returned with a large napkin which he handed to her. And stood next to her.

Slim Jem walked into the living room, with her shotgun, and stood in front of the kitchen doorway.

Rona told grandmother all that he had been told.

"Um ah," she grunted, lurching to her feet.

She walked slowly over and stopped to peer at the man on the couch. Her shapeless black dress seemed to suck up the light around her.

She leaned close and hissed something at him.

His eyes flew wide.

Then she thumped him on the forehead with the top of her hiking staff, driving him into the back cushion.

Turning, she looked at Rona.

"This one," she stated clearly, "is a Nightwalker. He thought to gain dark power from the bones of a young child. Pour some gasoline on him and light him up!"

She smiled at Slim Jem and grunted, "Good breakfast, Tall Beauty."

She turned away and headed for the front door, waggling one arm at Charity Jane. The pair left the house, closing the door behind them.

Rona peered down at that guy. "Your choice. Gasoline, or, talk to me."

He dragged a chair over which he spun around and sat in, straddling it, arms folded over the back.

"Well . . . ?"

"Do not threaten me, else I will bring great and powerful dark upon you," growled the occupant of the couch.

Rona smiled at him. "Nope! Whatever you might believe and what I happen to believe are two different things." He looked sideways. "Henry, go fetch that gas can from Jem's garage."

Henry hurried into the kitchen and out the back door.

Rona pulled a cheap plastic lighter from his pocket and flicked it on. A small yellow flame danced at the end.

"Good to go," he stated.

"We," stated the old man firmly, "are on a mission to bring those from the other worlds to this one. My failure here will have no effect."

He yanked a hand from his pocket, tossed something into his mouth, swallowed, jumped up, and ran for the door.

And collapsed halfway there.

Rona rolled the body over and looked at the face. *Well this guy was sorta dumb.*

Then he addressed the room. "I'll write everything up when it is morning and notify the state folk. Put the carcass somewhere that dogs can't get at it. They will probably want it, the state folk that is."

He headed for the door, stopped, turned, and smiled.

"Thanks Jem, for everything. And all the rest of you. I am going home and back to sleep."

She winked and smiled back. It was a very warm smile. Then she fetched his sandwiches and coffee and handed them to him.

He spun, walked out the front door, and disappeared into the night toward where he had parked his truck.

Not Good At All

Stream sat at the kitchen table, one hand curled around her large coffee mug. It was labeled, in large ornate script, *Good Job!* In the not too distance past the boss has given it to her after a particularly difficult report, one she had finally assembled into something that really made sense.

She was enjoying the early morning sun pouring through the kitchen window bouncing off the soft yellow walls, her coffee, and the odors of breakfast being prepared by Lou.

He was dressed in his usual casual attire, soft comfortable trousers, loose tan shirt, complete with a shoulder holster and gun. Never leave home without it, he had told her with a grin.

She was wrapped in a radiant yellow robe of some thick material which was showing signs of long and heavy use. She thought that she would wear it until it fell apart. As far as she was concerned it had many, many miles to go and there was absolutely no reason to buy something new.

"So partner," she asked, "what's cooking?"

Lou had agreed to fix breakfast as long as she took care of dinner.

"Ranch eggs, with tomatoes, onions, green chilies, hot sauce, and hash browns, sausage patties, toast. And jelly. Coffee, of course!"

"Sounds good to me." She laughed, a happy laugh, and added, "As long as you made lots."

"Sure." He was constantly amazed at her metabolic process, given how much she ate without gaining weight. Her father was tall and slim as she was, so maybe that explained it.

"So," he asked as he began to place platters covered with breakfast on the kitchen table, "what's on the schedule?"

"Same old, same old," she replied as she began to place large quantities of breakfast on her plate. "Two reports to put together. One large, one small. Go camping. Just the usual stuff." She shrugged and added, "Peace and quiet."

"Sure," he said.

Peace and quiet sounded good.

They ate breakfast, liberally dosing things, as required, with red salsa.

Then while Lou cleaned up the kitchen, Stream went down the hall to dress in her office clothes, essentially her usual camping attire, flannel shirt, jeans, comfortable shoes for the office and non-business activities in and about town. Her boots rode along in her truck.

She was done before he was.

So she helped dry things and put them away.

Lou opened the large gate in the thick and tall outside walls that ringed her property, as did most of the other properties in this older edge of town, and stood to one side as she backed her large, dust covered rig into the street, and waited while she closed and locked the gate before climbing back into the cab of the truck.

This was the oldest neighborhood of the town, dating back to the original, more or less, settlement. It was probably the quietist neighborhood in the town as well.

It was an area of narrow roads, no sidewalks or curbs, and no street lights. It was a place that was usually ignored by the city government. Everyone who lived here thought that was just fine.

Lou sat back and enjoyed the ride as Stream headed for their office as she turned here and there and finally parked in their parking spot in the very secure parking area.

"Just a couple of fairly simple, I was told, reports to put into shape," she said.

She looked over and laughed. "We can dawdle over lunch however we wish."

She opened her door and jumped down. It was a large truck after all.

They entered the building, passed through the security system and the watchful folk, strolled down the hall and around the corner to their office.

It was an office designed to do the job that they did. Several computers with large displays sat on work tables, a back room to take a cat-nap or to stay overnight in, if the work demanded it. Filing cabinets, a coffee maker, comfortable chairs, good lighting, and if they wished, music to listen to. Most of the walls were painted a soft white having just a faint touch of blue. One wall was painted a light yellow.

Rala had already started their coffee maker. She liked to get to work slightly before anyone else.

She had Aspergers, tended to prefer to not talk to most people, and had a two room office with no windows on the hall and heavy duty sound proofing. For her work she required no distractions of any kind.

Rala was one of the top analysts of the company. Her ability to concentrate on what ever data needed looking at and her ability to see connections others tended to miss in all that data made her very valuable for what the organization did.

Stream checked their in-box, a very large open tub mounted on a pedestal just inside the door to the office by the outside wall.

"OOOOP!" She lifted out several thick binders and expandable storage sleeves and dropped it all on one of the work tables.

"I guess," she shrugged, "we won't have all those casual lunches after all. This one is a biggie!"

"Yep." Lou shrugged off his jacket and hung it on a handy hook.

He had switched from carrying his gun in a jacket pocket to wearing it in a holster. He had decided that it would be better to be able to get at it easier, given some of the things that had happened in the not too distant past.

He sat at one of the computers and pulled up one of the folders of the two documents they were currently working on and looked at the display.

He started at the conclusion and then began to work through all the data presented, keying each bit to some sentence in the conclusions. Any sentence of the conclusion that couldn't be supported by data was marked for review in the overall discussion. Anything that could not be supported was due to be removed. If the conclusions, after all the removal, could not be supported then the entire project would usually be returned to the authoring agency to recheck the whole thing. It would be their problem to fix. Whether more research was to be done before that was up to Lou and Stream.

Stream, on her computer, opened a copy of the same materials and began to rewrite everything into normal everyday speech, removing jargon and replacing it with language that anyone could understand.

When they both had finished then they would stitch it all together into a coherent whole. And then reread it all over again, fixing whatever required fixing.

It was a process the pair had worked out on earlier projects.

It had improved final reports.

The recipients of those reports now stated how nice it was to read the final product without having to wade through jargon and overblown statements. It had made their activities easier in that they saw that they were being much more well informed.

It took Stream and Lou most of their work week to finish the two "small" reports.

On Friday they went out for a "casual" lunch having just turned in the final report product to those who would print and bind the several volumes of each report and then see to it that the reports were delivered into the correct hands.

Stream and Lou had put in long hours and had slept in the rooms attached to various of the offices that served such a need.

This time their casual lunch was at a neighborhood TexMex restaurant. There they ate their way through various of the entries and side dishes, accompanied by lots of salsa and beer.

Finally, several hours later, stuffed and relaxed, they climbed into Stream's truck and headed for her place.

Soon, they were sprawling on various pieces of furniture in the living room sipping a very dark and sturdy coffee as Stream pondered out loud various of the camping places that offered splendid isolation, peace, and quiet.

Lou made non-committal sounds now and then, just to show that he was paying attention.

The front door opened.

Lou's gun seemed to jump into his hand.

"Hey there," said Stream.

Lou's gun jumped back into its holster.

The pair that walked in were Lupe and her brother Luis, relatives of the elderly pair who lived just across the street. They kept an eye of Stream's place whenever she was not at home, regardless of the length of time she was away.

Stream headed for the kitchen and returned with two mugs of coffee which she handed to their visitors, then sat on the couch.

"What?" she asked them.

The pair took an appreciative sip from their mugs before they sat.

"Grandmother sent us," explained Lupe. "She thought that you ought to know."

"What?" asked Stream again.

"Two days ago," stated Luis.

"Late at night," added Lupe, "some stranger tried to snatch Chico as he was walking from his house to his Aunt's house. That large extended family tended to do that with the kids. They wander back and forth."

"Dee Dee heard his screams," added Luis, "and ran to the outside door and into the street. She told us that she saw a mob of dogs swarm over the kidnapper, mauling him." He looked at Stream. "Those dogs did not harm Chico."

Lupe shrugged. "That is what grandmother wanted you to know."

"Who?" asked Stream, "was he?"

Both shrugged.

"The kidnapper died. The cops are having trouble identifying him as he didn't have any identification of any kind in his pockets. He was dressed rather strangely. He had a owl skin, complete with feathers, attached to the back of his shirt, sorta like a small cape."

The pair stood, set their cups on a small table, and headed for the door.

"See ya, Stream," they said in unison as they left the house.

"Huh," stated Lou.

"Yep," agreed Stream, "kinna strange. This is a bad neighborhood to try things like that. Most folk here pay close attention to everything that goes on around the place. Wonder what that guy thought he was doing. Not good at all."

"Mob of dogs?"

She shrugged. "Sorta strange, also."

Then they talked about, and decided, where they would go camping.

An Epidemic?

The Chief of Police stared across his desk, a rather large and neat desk considering all the paperwork he had to deal with, at his best detective, not only considered the best by The Chief, but by all the other folk in the system. This was quite amazing given a department that was quite large, staffed by folk who generally had strong opinions about almost everything, especially things related to the police.

"Say again?" growled The Chief.

"Mrs. Van Den something or other just phoned and demanded immediate action."

"About?" prompted The Chief.

"Her son, aged eight, was camping in their backyard last night and has disappeared."

"Uh huh."

"The backyard fence is too high for her kid to climb. The only exit is through the house. The house is locked up tight at night, all night, with all manner of security devices. So, he couldn't disappear by himself."

"And they live where?"

"They live in that all so secure, all so private, all so expensive, all so gated development that went up a number of years ago. One road in, with gate and guards. High wall all around the development, unclimbable from either side, at least so say their brochures."

"Gumpf," observed The Chief.

"It is the same night," added Detective Matias Meredith, "as that attempt out on the Fringe, as most call the oldest and mostly neglected part of town. Only that snatcher was killed by a pack of dogs as was seen by a number of the locals. That part of town opens out onto the desert."

"Hum," grumbled The Chief, "that is two in one night."

"Yes. Both kids were the same age, more or less." Metias waggled one hand. "One seven years old, one eight years old, both male."

"Bad coincidence." The Chief leaned back in his chair. "Haven't had anyone that young disappear, or snatched, in, ummmm, ten years."

He frowned at his best detective. "Two in one night."

"Three."

"WHAT?"

"A young boy was reported missing from that sprawling housing out and around those large stores and the shopping mall, etc."

The Chief snatched his coffee cup and took a swallow.

"We having," he asked, "an epidemic?"

Matias shrugged.

"Go!" said The Chief, "see if you can find out anything useful. You better start with Mrs. Whosis first."

Matias spun on his heels and left the office. He already had a list of names and addresses of those that he would visit. He thought that he had better start with the wealthy first and try and stop any meddling they might think of with newspapers and political personages, distracting everyone and making his job hard, especially if they decided to start throwing around reward money for information.

He drove up to the heavy duty ornate gate, rolled down his window, showed his badge to the guard, one of the two, and told them who he wanted to speak to.

The guard stepped back inside their building, made a phone call, and raised the gate.

Detective Meredith drove in.

He didn't require directions. He knew where he was going.

Parking in the circular driveway, near the double wide front door, he got out and walked up to the entrance.

This was one of the most opulent dwellings in this area of opulent dwellings. Lots of glass, well maintained lawns and gardens, fancy and ornate this and that added to the house exterior.

He yanked his jacket into place and pushed the door bell button. He could have yanked on the bell pull cord hanging next to it, but didn't.

In a moment, one half of the great door swung open.

"Mariana."

"Matias."

She stepped back and waved him inside, leading him to a back room of glass walls and potted plants.

Two cups and a coffee container sat on the table.

She poured and waited for him to sit.

He did.

She handed him a cup and sat across from him.

He took a sip. It was delicious, as always.

Setting his cup down, he said, "Tell me."

She did. Carefully and with all the detail that she knew.

"Has anyone been in that yard since?"

"Just me." She stood and led him to the door that opened onto all that well mown grass and equally well attended flower beds. She waited in the doorway as he walked past and told him, "I will stay here."

He nodded and slowly, carefully walked along the edge

of the lawn and inspected the flower beds. The back sides of the three sided space was inclosed by a very tall wall.

He made three circuits of the space, two in one direction, one in the other. Then he walked just as slowly and carefully down the middle of the flower beds.

After his inspection, he walked over to one corner, and crouched, carefully parting some of the flowers. Standing up, he fished his cell phone free and made a call. Then he carefully backed away and walked back to the door.

"Footprints," he told her. "Someone not your son left them. Some of my people will arrive soon to take more photographs and make a casting of a footprint, at least as much as they are able to do."

He strode past her, picked up his coffee cup, murmured soft reassuring statements to Mariana, and drained the cup.

"Not much to go on," he told her.

Soon two folk dressed in white suits arrived to do their ever so careful inspection and data gathering.

When they finished, they came back and told him, "No blood out there."

The other held out a plastic evidence bag to Mariana. "Recognize this button?"

Mariana shook her head.

"That's good," he said. "Maybe we will be able to trace it."

Matias thanked them, stood, and told her, "We will be monitoring your phone for awhile, just in case."

She looked up at him. "Thanks, Matias."

He nodded. "I will let myself out. Lots of work to do."

He headed for the front door and his next stop.

He drove across town, over to the edge where the mall

and other large shopping outfits were located. He cut around all that enticement and entered the maze of streets that were the housing developments that curved around and up to all that shopping.

He noted that lots of the local residents walked along the streets to and from the various businesses.

It was interesting that many of the developers had created numbers of pocket parks, parks of one or two blocks in size, of mown grass with a baseball diamond here, a soccer field there, or just picnic tables and benches. All these parks had water fountains with doggy bowls at their bases.

Such things had obviously been part of the attraction for moving here as well as the close at hand shopping.

Matias checked his map and drove slowly through the road tangle created by each developer's idea of a proper road network that intersected the other developer's concept of a proper road network. The end result felt like a bit of a maze to travel through.

It took awhile but eventually he arrived at one of a number of identical houses along a road that edged the open space beyond the houses, streets, people, and parks.

In one direction lots of development, in the opposite direction, some houses, beyond them open space, random clumps of vegetation, and games trails often utilized by the local folk as hiking trails.

He parked in front of a dwelling painted a soft pastel blue. It stood out in a sea of housing painted green, or brown, or yellow.

He knocked on the front door and waited.

Eventually it opened.

"Mrs. Brownlee," he said, "I am Detective Meredith, might I come in and talk with you?"

She nodded and backed inside. "Come in."

She pointed at the living room and took a detour through the kitchen to pick up two cups and a container of coffee, coffee she had brewed right after he had phoned her about his coming visit.

They sat side by side on the short couch, cups and all on the table in front of them.

She poured both cups full and waited until he took a sip, then she did.

"Mrs. Brownlee," he repeated, "may I ask you some questions?"

"Carla," she replied. "Sure."

"First, tell me all you know, even if it is repetitious from what you told others. It is important for me to hear it."

She nodded.

She did.

Jerold, her son, often played in the backyard in the evening. Many times he would walk out on one of the trails for short walks. He was very comfortable being in the dark. When he didn't come back in, she assumed that was what he was doing, hiking out into the open space that bordered this part of the community.

When he failed to come into the house at his usual time, she waited, assuming that he had decided to walk further than normal. However, around midnight, she phoned the police. Two officers came out, made comforting noises, and left.

Matias nodded.

"May I," he asked, "wander around in your back yard to see whether I can find anything?"

She nodded.

"I will probably take a walk on that game trail some distance. But I will return and tell you what, if anything, that I find."

She nodded again, stood, walked over and opened the outside door, and said, "Through here."

He stood and walked outside.

Standing at the edge of the small concrete pad, he looked at the backyard. He examined the backyard. He studied the backyard.

Then he slowly walked around the edge of the neatly mown lawn passing the carefully tended flower beds.

Satisfied with his inspection he started, slowly, carefully, walking along that trail. Here and there he spotted the child's footprints. When he could no longer find any trace, he turned and walked back along one edge of the trail, checking the bare soil between the vegetation. As soon as he saw one of the child's footprints, he crossed over and started back up along the outside of the trail, studying the bare spaces between the vegetation.

He nodded, stopped, and pulled roll of red flagging from a jacket pocket and tied streamers around the spot where someone had stood, leaving their footprints. They were similar to those he had found earlier in the day.

Putting the roll back into his pocket, he took a small camera from another pocket, took a number of pictures, put the camera away, and slipped his cell phone from an inside jacket pocket, and made a phone call.

He headed back to the house, retrieved his coffee cup, and took a sip.

"A number of my people," he told her, "will shortly arrive. Please show them the trail. They have some work to do as I found some footprints that were not your son's. Some of those folk are going to hike that trail and see where it leads, see if they can find anything else."

He shrugged an apology. "At the moment that is all we

can do. Do you want me to wait until they arrive?"

She shook her head and murmured, "No, I will be all right."

He nodded.

"Thank you for the coffee."

In his car he headed back toward the center of town and the coroner's office.

But first, he stopped at a small café and ordered a quick lunch.

Soon, he walked down those familiar stairs.

"Hello, Ned. Show me that dog mangled body from the fringe. I also want to see whatever he was wearing on his feet."

"Over here, Matias." Ned Hawkins tugged his white jacket into place and led him to the appropriate drawer and pulled it out and dragged the cloth from the body.

Matias looked at it. There were bite marks on both arms and legs, the throat had been tore out.

"The cops said that the neighbors told them that a mob of dogs did this. It was dark so they couldn't see what kinds of dogs they were. From the bite marks I would see not dogs but coyotes."

"Why?"

"If it was some sort of loose dog pack, I would assume that it consisted of a variety of different types, umm, breeds of dogs. Modern dog heads, depending on the breed, come in a number of shapes and configurations. Thus I would expect the bites marks to show that kind of variety. It is not there. All the bites look pretty much the same as to configuration. Thus, perhaps, coyotes."

Matias nodded and pulled the cloth back in place.

Ned slid the drawer closed.

"His things are back this way."

Opening a cabinet, he offered Matias his pick of several large plastic evidence bags.

Matias took one and looked at the footwear. They were soft leather that pulled halfway up the calf of the leg and tied in the front. The bottoms were smooth, no tread of any kind. The footprints they would have made would have been similar to the footprints he had found in two different places.

He looked at Ned. "Can you tell me anything about this footwear?"

Ned nodded. "Indian gear of some kind. At least made by an Indian of some kind. You can buy these during a lot of the craft fairs."

"Thanks, Ned."

Matias headed back to tell The Chief all that he had found. It was not much, pretty much still a mystery. But they had a few small hints to go on.

Vision Quest

As things often happened, Stream received a phone call before they could leave her house on a planned camping trip.

She listened, nodded to herself, hung up, and sighed.

"What?" asked Lou.

"The boss has a, ah, as he stressed it, a very, very large and complicated project which now requires the final report to be made. He said that he thought this final report would take, at least, a week if we put in long hours. He also said that we could take however much time off we wanted afterwards."

She smiled and pointed out to Lou that this was the first time, ever, that the boss had done anything like this. So, this indicated that this project was very important, more so than anything that they had previously worked on.

"Ready for this, Lou?"

"As ever." He nodded and headed for the outside door, saying as he did, "Shall we?"

She laughed and followed him.

As soon as she drove her large truck out onto the narrow street, Lou closed the heavy gate in the wall, locked it, checked that it was locked, then clambered into the front seat.

"Wonder what this is all about?" he said.

"We shall see," she replied, "we shall see."

The big machine hurtled down the street, headed for their office.

After parking in the secure parking area, they passed through the security space and the security personnel and walked down the hall and into their office. And much to their surprise they found Rala, The Squirrel, sitting at one of the large computer tables, drinking coffee. She had started Stream's coffee maker right after the boss had told her that Stream and Lou would shortly be in their office to work on "that" project.

"I used your coffee," Rala carefully explained. "It is better than anything found in any of the other offices or the break room."

She smiled at Stream, filled two cups, and handed them around.

"Thanks, Rala," said Stream, inhaling the aroma, then taking a sip.

Rala pushed two thick folders across the table at Stream.

"I made these," Rala explained, "an overview and a suggested structure for the final reports."

She pointed at the four very large boxes stacked on Stream's desk and stated, "Just lots and lots and lots of reports and data."

She shoved a third folder at Stream, her brows wrinkling as she murmured softly, "This is what I saw in all that data."

Rala had a unique skill to do that, to find correlations in masses of data.

She drained her coffee cup, set it on top of the third folder, and stood, announcing firmly, "I am going home and watch movies." Tears began to pour down her face.

"I am," she whispered harshly, "going to take two days off." She jabbed a finger at the boxes and the folders, and murmured, "This is very, very ugly."

She lurched forward and wrapped her arms around Stream, hugging her tight.

Stream gasped softly. She knew that Rala hated to be touched.

Carefully, ever so gently, Stream patted her on the back, and whispered to her, "Take all the time off you wish, Rala, all the time off you wish. Just phone if there is anything you want me to do. O.K.?"

Rala pushed back, gave Stream a quick nod of her head, hurried from the office and down the hall.

Stream swivelled her chair around and dropped into it, took a great swallow from her cup, and stared at Lou.

"What?"

"Lou, nothing has ever bothered Rala like that before. Nothing! Ever!" She indicated the boxes and folders. "What the hell is this?"

She jabbed a forefinger at the three folders. "You read those two while I read the third. Then we will find a restaurant where we may be very private and have something to eat and talk about whatever this is."

He nodded, took the two folders and sat in a chair in a far corner from the office door and began to read.

She leaned back, feet and legs on the desk top, refilled coffee cup within reach, and began to read Rala's findings.

What on earth had she seen that had caused such a reaction?

When she had finished, she sat and stared out the large glass window of her office and at the empty corridor beyond. She waited, seeing in her mind what Rala had described.

She waited for Lou to finish.

Uncounted time passed. Lou stood, dropping the two folders with a heavy thump on the computer desk where he sat.

Clearing his throat three times before he could speak, he rasped, "Let's go."

The owner of the restaurant gave them his backroom for themselves, setting two glasses and a bottle of wine on the table where they sat, before backing away and closing the door. Stream had talked with him and he would see that no one would enter for how ever long she wished.

After they had eaten a quiet meal, pizza covered with a large number of different topping, and drank most of the wine, Lou nodded across the table at her.

"That bunch," he stated, "all ought to die!"

Stream nodded. "Not our call."

He refilled his glass and drained it.

"I know. This is going to be a hard one to work on."

She stood. "I'll have dinner and breakfast ordered for as many days as we require. The owner will make special menus. We will eat out, just to clear our heads."

While Lou waited in the truck, Stream talked with the owner, a long-time friend.

Then they went back to her office.

It took them eight long days to put the several reports together before they finally handed everything to the folks in printing and binding to do their work.

She drove them to the restaurant and saw that the owner was well compensated. Then she drove to a restaurant/bar in a less well repaired neighborhood. The bar was filled with mostly males of a rugged appearance who watched the pair as they entered and found a place to sit. Then they went back to their conversations having decided that it was best to do that. The expression on that guy's face was a storm waiting to settle on something.

Lou and Stream sat in a corner booth, backs to the wall, ate dinner, not really caring what it was, and were working on their second pitcher of dark beer, when a young man stepped inside and looked around.

He looked across the dingy room and walked in a straight

line to them. The inhabitants parted before him. They saw something that they decided was not to mess with.

When he reached their table, he handed Stream a large manila envelope, and departed.

She opened it and withdraw a single sheet of heavy bond paper.

"Cohan," she said.

Lou nodded. He remembered.

Cohan was from one of the many tribes which he never identified as to his membership, was a well know artist whose paintings, when he chose to put one up for sale, caused a bidding war. No one knew how much money he made or how much he had. He lived in a rather normal looking house in a rather normal looking neighborhood.

Stream had told Lou that Cohan was what folk in the tribes call a seer. She explained that it meant, in a loose translation, one who sees/knows things that normal folk can not. Along with that talent, Cohan concocted an alcoholic beverage that was known widely for its effect on any who imbibed it. The one, and only, time Lou and Stream had done that, they had both wound up flat of their backs in her living room, he on the floor, she on the couch which she had managed to reach as she fell. And that was due to a rather small quantity that they had sipped from a single bottle.

Stream reached across the table and handed Lou the drawing and watched his face.

It was a three-dimensional drawing of an arroyo, twisting and turning into the distance before it curved toward the right hand side of the paper and out of sight.

A dotted line indicated the path that was being followed by a small cat as that path wandered back and forth across the arroyo and up onto a bench and then down again.

Lou recognized some of the landmarks. He and Stream had walked that path and found the dead body of Fergy which had led them deeper and deeper into the workings of a large scale criminal organization. Much of the work that Lou and Stream had done had helped land a lot of folk of that organization in jail.

Fergy had been known as a money handler, that is, someone who knows how to see that it comes from over there and that it gets to somewhere else safely. He was very, very good at doing that. For Fergy it had been a very good money making process. Lots and lots of money. He called it a business. Fergy had a rare talent for things like that and certain folk had paid generously for him to do just that. Until he died.

Ornate script ran across the bottom of the drawing.

The old ones call the cat to come and listen.

Lou knew that when Cohan sent a drawing like this to Stream that the cat figure represented her.

Stream emptied the pitcher into her glass, took a swallow, and stared at Lou, blank faced.

"What?"

"I didn't think that things," she said, then emptied her glass, "could get any worse."

"Huh?"

"You don't have to come."

"Partner," he stated, "where you go, I go. There is no argument about that."

She nodded, stood, dropped a handful of bills on the table top.

"We will leave in the morning after we pack our gear. We will have to take enough food to carry us over twelve days, that gives us a two day of a just-in-case leeway. Take the biggest gun you own."

Lou almost winced at that suggestion.

Now what where they getting into?

After rattling along and over a number of marginal roads, wheel ruts and barely visible indications of past travel, Stream parked, on a bare spot, turned off her rig, jumped out, pocketed her keys, and began to unload their gear from the back.

She pointed, as she had done the last time they had been here.

"There is a trail right there, that slight notch, remember it?"

Lou nodded.

She started off.

"Another nice day for a walk."

The sun rose higher and began to glare down on them and everything else.

The trail pitched over the edge through the slight notch and began to wander along the side slope until it reached the bottom of the wide and dry arroyo.

Everything in sight was a light yellow mixed with soft rust brown and all shades in between. A few bushes grew here and there, most were dead.

"Desolate spot."

She laughed.

"What?"

"That's what you said before."

When they reached the bottom they could see the traces of faint animal tracks as the trail headed upstream, upstream that is if there had been water flowing down here. The animal tracks had come and gone in both directions.

"There are a few long ago abandoned cabins, of a sort, up this way, abandoned ruins, a couple of poor attempts at mining. That stuff reflects the history of this area."

Lou nodded. He remembered but felt that she had a need to talk about things not related to what they were really doing.

Slowly, ever so slowly, as they hiked along, the side walls began to rise and the width of the arroyo narrowed.

Stream pointed up at one bench.

"First stop."

Lou looked. He could just see a bit of grey weathered wooden something up there.

Stream led him up the correct trail.

Once they had walked to the top they could see that the structure was still standing, more or less. It appeared as if the only reason that it had not collapsed into a mass of twisted timber was the very large boulder that it had slumped against. She led him around and to the only doorway. The door had fallen outward and lay in front of the structure. Lou peered through the remains of the only window, it had fallen inside, and could see that no one was at home.

"Long time since anyone was here."

"Yep. We will just walk along up here for a bit." She pointed. "You can see that next structure from here."

Lou started in the direction indicated, squinted, his eyes scanning back and forth.

"Ahhh," he said. "It looks to be in even worse shape than when we were here before."

"Yep." She strolled off. "No hurry."

When they arrived at the collapsed structure they found that only the portion of one corner was still intact. It made a rather small cave like space amidst the jumbled weathered wood building remains.

Stream shrugged off her backpack, retrieved her flashlight, knelt, and shined it inside the dark space.

"Rodent nest, otherwise empty. Same old, same old."

She stood, replaced her flashlight, and swung her pack into place.

"The next stop is that old mining attempt on the other bench."

Lou followed her as she strolled along near the edge of the arroyo.

"Did you see those tiny flowers back there?" he asked.

She laughed. "Yep."

He was getting better and better at seeing the environment in detail.

Finally she clambered down the side and led him up the other side of the now very narrow arroyo. As they reached the top, Lou cleared his throat, loudly.

"How about we stop for a snack?"

She pointed.

"There?"

"There."

When they finally arrived at "there" Lou could see that the arroyo bent sharply to the right, narrowed, and then broadened out again.

"The rock right here is a narrow dike of hard stuff," explained Stream. He nodded and headed up to the top of the arroyo side wall.

Up there, she walked over and sat. "Pull up a boulder, we can snack for a bit." She smiled at him as he did. Sit on one of the right-sized boulders for sitting upon.

As she opened something and took a bite, she mumbled around the crumbs, "Welcome to The Little Wonder Mine picnic area." She indicated the framing around the dark opening.

"They went back a couple of hundred feet or so. Their ore cart is parked back there on the rails."

Lou looked around. One tiny, weather beaten but was still somehow standing shack with a stove pipe still sticking up through the roof. The framing around the tunnel opening was large, rough cut timbers. He could see more of the same disappearing into the gloom of the tunnel. The narrow gauge rail ran from the tunnel to the edge of the arroyo apparently to dump debris over the edge. Looking over the edge he could see that heavy runoff, or flash floods, had carried it all away.

"Pretty quiet out here."

"Yep," she agreed. "Wait here, be right back."

She took her flashlight and headed into the darkness. "Just checking for footprints."

In a moment she strode back outside.

"No visitors of the human kind."

She checked the shed, came back, and picked up her pack, flashlight once again properly stowed.

"Ready?"

"Sure." He stood, yanked his pack up and into place, and looked for any sign of structures upstream, and shrugged.

"Spick and span."

"Some distance from here you'll see the ruins, dwellings of the long ago folk. Not a bad place to camp when you are prepared to do that."

They dropped down into the arroyo and trudged onward.

Lou thought the grade seemed to be getting, ever so gently, steeper. He remembered that and looked at the side walls and noted the scoring way above their heads. The water must really roar down through here when it rains higher up. He checked the piece of sky that he could see ahead of them. It was a clear blue, not a cloud to be seen. From here.

"I checked the weather forecasts," she said, noticing the direction he was staring. "Nothing to worry about."

It was a long walk to the ruins. This gave him lots of time to examine his environment, and, ever so carefully, his boss. Being out here seemed to be having a positive effect.

She was a very relaxed person in her own unique way and obviously athletic, the way she moved. She carefully kept herself unknown but as she talked about this or that he got a peek, now and then, of the real person behind the carefully controlled mask, the person kept ever so carefully out of sight. There was so much more to her than he suspected anyone really knew but he was getting to know her more and more the longer they worked together.

And that was all to the good.

As they rounded another of the bends in what was becoming a rather twisting arroyo, she pointed.

"Up there. We have to follow that game trail and then you will see them."

She started up the game trail as it worked its way to the top.

They stopped, giving Lou, once again, a chance to look over the series of stacked stone structures.

"Quiet a complex." He walked toward a corridor that appeared to lead into the center of the cluster.

She led him past several of the buildings and stopped next to a mostly complete structure.

"We can camp here and stroll out in the morning."

She shrugged off her pack and began to take out what was needed.

After they ate dinner, while the light was still bright enough, they cleaned what needed to be cleaned, laid out their sleeping gear, and played a few games of cribbage.

The sky darkened and they put away the game. She had won all the games.

She sat on the spread out sleeping bag and pad and leaned back against the handy wall.

"Nice view from here. Think?"

Lou smiled as he spread out his stuff.

"Yes. It is." It had been the last time as well.

He jerked his thumb over his shoulder.

"Have you hiked further up?"

"Nope. We are headed into terra incognita for me."

"Oh boy," he laughed, "an adventure!"

"Let's hope not. Lou?"

"What?"

"I sent a memo to the boss about that last job."

"Oh?"

"I told him that the mess was because that agency had been dragging their feet and dodging the problem until it became such a disaster they couldn't ignore it any longer. I told him that I thought that they had been playing politics instead of doing the job that they were supposed to be doing."

"Sure."

"I also stated that if that crowd were ever to sent another thing like that to us that I would refuse to work on it, essentially covering their ass. That is not what we are supposed to be doing! If he tries to force me to work on something like that again, I will quit the company. He knows that if I quit that he would loose Rala as well as some of the other folk as well."

"And me," stated Lou. "I think you were correct to tell him that."

"You wouldn't have to leave."

"Partner, I was hired specifically to work with you, just

you. Therefore, you leave, I leave. Simple."

Stream sat up, she had been lying on her back watching the stars come out, and stared at him. They were close enough that she could.

"You were hired specifically to work with me?"

"Yep."

"Why?"

"Given the last several, ah, helpers that you had, the boss was worried about your safety and felt that I was someone, ah, more appropriate for that job."

"My safety?"

"Yep."

"He didn't tell me that."

"Probably afraid that you would punch him, or something."

"Sooooo," she snarled, "you are my watch dog?"

"Nope. I am your partner, partner." He laughed. "Beside, we work very well together. But, if someone needs to be shot, well partner, they will get shot."

She flopped back and rolled on her side to look at him in the ever fading light.

"You are carrying a different gun?"

"Yep."

"How come?"

"Ahhhhhhh, you mentioned it. I just thought I ought to be ready, ummmm, well, if we might need it. Hardly ever carry this one." He sighed. "Beside you suggested it," he repeated.

"Ummmmm," she replied.

"Stream, this thing," he said softly, "will kill anything that gets shot. Ehh, I was worried, sorta, that's all, especially when you suggested that I carry the biggest gun that I owned."

"O.K., partner," she mumbled as she fell asleep, "you fix

breakfast."

"Sure."

She seemed to have an on and off switch. She fell asleep within a few breathes.

It took him awhile to do the same thing.

In the early morning light she woke to soft metallic sounds. Lou was making breakfast.

She sat up, yanked on her boots, stood and walked out and around one of the stacked stone structures, and shortly returned.

"What's for breakfast?" she asked.

"Powdered eggs and instant coffee."

"Yum yum."

She sat. He handed her a metal plate and a cup, both already filled.

He stood and rummaged around in his pack and extracted a small paper bag.

Turning back, he set a cinnamon roll on her plate and took a bite from the other one.

"Surprise!" He smiled at her.

"Yep." She smiled back.

He sat. "Not too heavy, and besides, we just lightened the load, a bit."

"You are just full of surprises," she mumbled around a mouthful of cinnamon roll.

"Sometimes. Sorta like my partner." He poured coffee into her cup and his, emptying the small pot.

After they cleaned their camp, what little it needed, and hefted their packs into place, they started up the narrow trail, Stream leading the way.

A short way up the trail she stopped, yanked out Cohan's

map and unfolded it.

She pointed. "Not too far that way, the map shows a water source off the trail and aways up the slope. We should fill our water bottles there. The map shows other sources but we ought to play it safe. We are in no hurry."

"Sure."

On they walked, ever higher as the land lifted and the arroyo sank deeper below grade.

They stopped for a quick lunch and trudged ever onward.

"There is a small ruin of some kind indicated on the map. We can camp there. Hopefully it is not too fallen in."

She gestured at the arroyo ahead of them.

"See that bend way ahead. When we walk around it, we walk off Cohan's map" She shook her head. "And I have no idea why he stopped his drawing there."

Not longer after that conversation they walked up a rise and then down into a broad swale formed by runoff.

Sitting next to the steep sided creek bed there was a small stacked stone structure.

The roof was gone, the only doorway short and narrow.

They peeked inside at the jumble and decided to camp near one of the walls. If a wind storm should come their way, they could retreat inside and hunker down until it passed. Otherwise, outside felt more comfortable to them.

"Second day," she said as she cooked dinner, such as it was, being dehydrated this and that.

"Counting?"

"Yep. Three more days along this trail and we stop and camp and search the area for one day. If we can't find whatever it is that we are supposed to find, we turn around and head back. That is six days in, five days out, and one day in reserve.

I am not going to be out here without supplies."

"Yep." Lou yanked out his pistol and began to check it for dirt and dust. He stuffed it back into his holster satisfied that it was good to go.

"Doesn't look any bigger than the one you usually carry."

"Partner, this gun and the cartridges that I carry and loaded it with will blow a four-inch hole in anything."

She stared at him.

"Why I carry the other one. But out here," he waved one hand at their surroundings, having set his plate down, " I thought that taking prisoners might not work all that well. You are nervous, so I am nervous. Spooky unknown and all that."

She nodded and ate dinner.

"If I say fire, do. If I say don't fire, don't. O.K.?"

"Yep." He held up one finger. "But, if something large, mean, and nasty, is trying to get you, I will shoot it!"

"Good enough."

She checked the light of evening approaching. "We can play a couple of games before it gets too dark."

Lou cleared what little needed to be cleared away while she dug the game out of her pack.

He lost, both games.

Morning.

The usual breakfast of powdered eggs and instant coffee.

The trail that they still hiked along wandered along the edge of the arroyo as it narrowed, as the gradient became steeper. The water course here began to take on the appearance of a rocky outwash and less like the wide arroyo it was back in the flatter country below.

Vegetation, trees and shrubs, were beginning to crowd the edges of the water course. The trail worked its way around and between dense pockets of growth.

"Damn!" growled Stream as she stepped around a large thicket.

There was a branch in the water course.

The large branch ran, more or less, straight ahead.

The smaller headed uphill at a much steeper angle. It seemed to have ripped straight down the slope from somewhere higher.

"Ummmm?"

"We'll follow the trail until it is time to camp, then we throw the dice, or something. Looking at the ground here there are certainly no indications as to which way we ought to go."

"Sure. However."

"What?"

"We don't have any dice to throw, not unless we use those in the game." He laughed.

So did Stream.

Lou nodded.

Much better.

They followed the trail until everything around them was casting long shadows. Then they camped.

She cooked dinner. The same stuff as before.

As they ate, they discussed, now what?

"Ummmmm?" asked Lou.

"What?"

"Well," he began, "you are the cat in Cohan's drawing. Anyone whispering in your ear, giving suggestions as to which way we should go?"

"Nope."

"Ah, well. Care for a game before it gets too dark?"

They played.

Lou lost.

He woke to the unusual sounds of Stream making breakfast.

As soon as they ate, packed everything, and heaved their packs into place, she said, "I think we ought to go back to that junction and follow that cut up the mountain side."

"Someone whisper in your ear?"

"Nope. Just have a feeling."

"Thrust your feeling."

They headed back.

They ate lunch at the intersection, drank some water, and looked up the slope.

"We're not going to cover as much ground climbing up that."

She nodded.

"We finish today. Then one more day. Nothing there, we can get back down in a day and head back. We can only go one more day and camp and search around. Then we are out of time and we head back regardless of anything."

"Sure."

"If we don't find anything," she grumbled, "then Cohan can draw a better map!"

They started up.

As they had thought, it was slow.

Late in the day they walked from a layer of trees and into a tiny meadow whose one edge was the gully.

"Camp here," she said, dumping her pack. "Nice spot."

"Fine by me." Lou dropped his pack and stretched. "Other than going straight up, it is not tooooo bad."

Stream fished a pair of binoculars from her pack, walked to the edge of the gully and slowly scanned up the slope.

Then she pointed. "Way up there is a dark spot where the ground gets kinna vertical. This cuts veers to the left, near there.

We should be able to get up there by late afternoon."

"Sure." He began to take out stuff for dinner.

"Up there," she explained, "is the first thing different in all that environment that we have walked through."

"Sure." He started their tiny cook stove and began making dinner. "You bring a camera?"

"Yep. Very small, very light, but it will do."

He handed her a plate and a cup. And laughed. "Eat hardy!"

Dawn flooded their spot with bright light.

Routine was routine.

    Cook. Eat. Pack.

And they were on their way.

    Up the mountain.

"Baa, baa," baa'd Lou.

"What?"

"Mountain goat." He laughed as he hiked his pack into a better position.

"At least the packs are lighter," he observed. "Good thing you eat so much."

She turned and kicked a small rock at him.

He watched it as it tumbled into the narrow wash.

"There is water up there."

"What?"

"There is," he explained, "a small amount of green growth in this wash. It appears to be greener further up."

"Good."

Up they went.

    Up.

    And up.

        And up.

Until they arrived.

"Wow," said Lou.

The dark spot had become a long depression in a rocky face that had been exposed by long ago erosion. It was about ten to twelve feet deep. The overhang had kept most of the weathering to the lower edge of the back face.

Rock fall and erosion from above had created a narrow flat space in front of the depression.

Lou stared at the back wall.

It was decorated.

The back wall was decorated with stylized figures of people, animals, intermingled with geometric designs of many varieties.

"Here we camp," announced Stream, dumping her pack, fishing her small camera out.

"Gimme your water bottles and the water filter, I'll see if there is enough water running through that greenery to fill them."

She handed him her bottles and the filter and began to take pictures of the back wall.

Lou scrambled down into the erosional feature caused by runoff and began to push the vegetation aside.

"Bingo! Found a small trickle," he called. "It'll work."

"Good." She walked back and forth, taking more pictures, recording the entire back wall.

Eventually they set up camp, fixed and ate dinner, and relaxed. They both felt that they had found what they had been searching for.

"Lou?"

"Ummm?"

"Don't shoot anything, no matter how bizarre. I don't want to damage the glyphs."

"Sure."

They played a number of games of cribbage.

Lou actually won two games.

The sun dropped behind their mountain and darkness swarmed up the slope.

Given that they felt they had arrived at the spot where they were supposed to be, they decided to go to sleep early and get up late and rested.

Her eyes popped open.

It was dark.

Almost.

There was a thin sliver of light on the outer edge of the cavern. The moon was high enough to pour illumination into the canyon and touch that spot and wash soft light over everything in the front third of the great open space.

Then she realized that the moon wasn't the only light source.

Some of the petroglyphs were glowing, a very soft yellow glow.

O.K., here we go again.

She sat up, and looked over. Lou was sitting up, carefully watching. He checked to see whether she was doing anything. Then watched and waited, waiting for her directions.

Two of the glowing petroglyphs seemed to float free of the wall and drift toward them, growing larger and larger as they approached.

The two figures now stood at the foot of their sleeping bags, staring at them.

A soft mist oozed from them and wrapped around until only a tall column of shimmering grey stood there.

The fog faded away and they stood looking at them. Two human appearing individuals, apparently human, dressed in strange garb.

The one wore a dark mask helmet with yellow, round painted eyes with great dark pupils. The hair style on the mask suggested that she was female. She wore a dark blue skirt with a great cape like garment over her shoulders that hung below her knees. She held a round gourd on a stick in her right hand and a strung bow in her left.

The other figure was obviously male, bare to the waist. He, like the woman, held the same sort of gourd device in his right hand and a strung bow in his left. On his head he wore a very stylized dog-like mask that covered his entire head.

The pair stood perfectly still, and now watched her.

Stream frowned, just a little.

Same pair as the last time. Now what? What did Cohan think he was doing sending her and Lou here?

Each of the figures shook their gourd rattles. And stopped.

"I am," said a deep female voice, a deep elder female voice, "called He'e'e in my people's tongue, a female warrior. In the very long ago I defended my people."

She shook her rattle again, and stopped.

"You are now my warrior, Stream The Warrior, Stream Wolf Daughter. We," she gestured at her companion, "have seen this. We have seen you grow into who you were to become. It is so!"

She held up the hand clenching the rattle to stop the questions she could see forming on Stream's face.

"Wolf Daughter, you, with your abilities, have been called!"

She waggled her hand toward the open space downhill.

"Out there are dark believing beings who wish to bring back what should not be brought back! It is a false belief yet one capable of great ill. It is not a thing for us! It is a thing for you to get rid of! It is so!"

She looked at the other, who nodded.

"I am," rasped a male voice, "called Poko in my people's tongue. The first domestic dog was my doing. Before they were dogs they were wolves. As the dog serves my people by being his friend, so the wolves-in-spirit will serve you as your's. This you know."

He shook his rattle, and stopped.

"Wolf Daughter have no fear!" The rattle holding hand waggled toward the open space below, then at Lou. "We see your companion, The Wolf Guardian. This one will protect! It is so!"

"Out there is a dark thing! It is a dark false belief causing great ill. It is not a thing for us! It is a thing for you to get rid of! It is so!"

"Now sleep," said the pair in unison. "Enjoy the peace and quiet of this place. It is a special place for us, it is now a special place for you."

The pair faded away and the only light that she could see was the narrow sliver of moon light at the edge of the cavern.

Stream slipped down and back into her sleeping bag and lay on her back staring up into the darkness where the cavern roof was.

Was what she had just experienced real, or just her imagination hard at work for some strange reason.

She turned her head and checked on Lou. He had his hands folded back under his head as he was staring up at the night sky.

She fell asleep.

They slept late, as planned.

Stream prepared breakfast, such as it was, once again powdered eggs and instant coffee.

As they ate, Lou looked up from his plate at her.

"What?"

"That is more than a little hard to believe," he said.

"I suppose."

"But it happened."

"Yep."

"Those two knew you?"

"Yep."

He refilled her cup, then his, emptying the small pot.

"Now what?"

"Now we head on back down and out. It is a long walk back. But our packs will just get lighter and lighter. We can stroll, not hurry."

"Yep."

Days later they drove into her place. She hurried into the house to phone the boss and to tell him that they would be out-of-the-office for a number of days more.

Lou closed and locked the heavy gate in the wall and walked inside the house.

As he stepped inside, she said, "I am first in the shower. You wanna start a real meal and a real pot of good coffee?"

Stream started down the hall, calling back, "Don't worry. I have a very large hot water heater!"

Lou headed for the kitchen.

Lots of hot water sound good.

A Long Loud Sigh

His secretary heard him sigh as he set down Stream's memo.

His secretary heard him as he made a decision.

As he passed her desk, he said as he opened the door to the hall, "Going to stroll around for awhile."

Ignatius Willum Ranpan began to wander the halls of the organization, the company recently renameded *ReVal* (Research & Evaluation), deep in thought.

He smiled slightly as he wandered. He knew that his organization was as unique as the people who worked for it.

The company had been designed to do research on any problem that the various legal agencies might submit to it, with one caveat, of all the programs suggested, the company would select from four to six to work on at that time. The company staff would work on these for as long as it took to reach an end point prior to releasing a report. They would use whatever research methods they felt were appropriate. Once that final report, or reports, were delivered, the company would never be identified in any manner whatsoever as the place from which that report came. Any breach of this by the agency would forever put that agency outside the pale as far as the company was concerned. And no manner of waving the flag or any thing else would change that.

So, he wandered the halls of the company deep in thought and pondered what else, if anything, needed doing. Stream's memo had raised an interesting dilemma.

I.W., as he was known outside the company, the boss (lack of a capitalized title was a deliberate statement on his part) as he was known inside the company.

As he strolled, smiling at this or that staff member passing in the halls, he thought deeply about the criteria had established for the function of the company as it worked for the various organizations it had been created to help.

Stream's memo just before she left for a extended camping trip had been a surprise. He was used to her taking camping trips whenever she felt the need. And now he was no longer worried for her safety. Not with Lou as her partner as a, more or less, constant companion. It would take a very large number of people working in a closely coordinated manner to harm her. Maybe.

He nodded to himself. Stream was correct. When he had started this company, all those organizations had been told the ground rules. There would be no games playing allowed.

He frowned darkly at nothing in particular. He had know the head of that organization for a long, long time, and in the past he had advised him a number of times. Something had changed out there. It was time to find out what.

He opened the door to Meeting Room 1 and walked in. The two best researchers he had ever heard of looked up and waited. They were now part of the organization.

One was dressed in a suit and tie, the other was wearing thrift shop inexpensive.

Periscope's shirt was covered with red and yellow flowers. He had dropped out of society and legally changed his name

He had never earned anything other than the grade of A through high school. Then he had enrolled in a number of different colleges and universities. He had no problem getting into anything that he applied for. In those places he took whatever courses that interested him, getting nothing but A's. Finally in a big time university, his view of the place, the psychology types convinced him to let them give him a series of tests. What happened was not what those researchers thought would happen. He zipped through every test that they gave him, including all the egghead mensa super brain things. He blew through them as fast as he could read them. They gave up. What they found out, so to speak, was that this guy was someone that they couldn't measure, other than, as far as they could figure out, is that he was some sort of super genius.

He was, as well, a very large person who dwarfed most of the folk who met him, including his associate sitting next to him.

Dr. Harris, a Ph.D. in those subjects which he had studied, could only be described as Mister Clean, a professor type with a number of degrees. He had opened his research endeavors a number of years back. He was considered to be one of the best. He lived well, he dressed well, he ate well. His house, in one of the more upscale neighborhoods, was nicely furnished, good art on the walls, fancy kitchen.

They were a contrast in life style and personalities.

As the boss sat down across the table from them, Dr. Harris straightened his tie, a little. Periscope smiled.

"Gentlemen," said I.W., "You two are the best of the best of the best researchers, apparently in the world."

Dr. Harris smiled, slightly. Periscope laughed, a deep laugh that rolled up from his thick chest.

"Butter, butter, butter," suggested Periscope.

The boss shook his head.

"Nope. It was merely an observation based on a rather extensive research of my own as well as your past endeavors."

He handed each a copy of Stream's memo and explained, "This is just for your information." He handed them another sheet of paper.

"This is who and what I want to know about!"

Periscope rapidly scanned his sheet.

Dr. Harris carefully read what he had been handed.

"This will be fun." Periscope beamed at the boss.

Dr. Harris shrugged. "It will be very tricky to keep him and them from realizing what we are doing."

I.W. nodded. "But?" he urged.

"But I am sure that we can do it. Time table?"

"None," stated the boss. "I want to know. Take your time, be as slow and careful as you think you need to be. Talk to Francis and tell him whatever you might require. He will see that you have it."

He stood and held up one hand, palm facing them. "This is a secret between just the three of us, what you are about to do."

They nodded.

Keeping, or finding, secrets, is what they did, as the boss had said, better than anyone else.

Keeping Track

Now they were gathered on a dark, moonless night, some of them.

Now they were here, on a dark moonless night, some of them.

They sat in a row, three figures, sitting on the hard packed dirt floor of the tall cylinder of carefully constructed stone.

To one side of them, a small fire, of very dry wood, burned in the round fire pit.

Each of the men wore loose capes draped over their shoulders made from the pelts of their spirit animals, signifying the one that had come to them in their early years.

Now having their own place, their own place of mystery and power, they had somewhere to keep their things, the things that friends and neighbors could not accidently find, accidently stumble over, and bring to their owner a slow death.

For the first time ever, they felt safe in their knowledge, the knowledge they had worked so hard to acquire, here in the spell of the swelling power that was to come.

This night, as on nights before, they would sing, feeling the power of the songs that they sang.

Here they sat, bodies decorated with paint, wearing masks and jewelry, feeling the power of their animal souls.

The sing would take most of the night.

Before sunrise they would leave and scatter, careful to

leave no trace. They would scatter, back to their homes and their lives, just one among the many.

Near one wall ran a line of small water rounded stones.

Behind the line sat two pottery bowls, one was a deep black, the other a light tan.

The eldest of the three, the one who had organized their endeavor, the one who had brought their small group into a unified existence, the one who had planned and planned, and directed the activities of the others, looked at that line of stones before them, and said, "Two have died."

He set two of the stones in the black bowl.

"Three have succeeded."

He placed three stones in the tan bowl.

He looked at the others.

"The children are well and are being taken care of by a special man in a special place. As each one still out there succeeds, that child will join the others. Only until all are finished with this first phase of our sacred work, will we begin the next step, the one that will enhance our powers to the level that we require. When that has been accomplished, then we will call forth those who have so long ago lived in our past worlds."

He looked from face to face. "Nothing should be rushed. All must be done carefully and with great thought. Haste only leaves openings for failure or discovery. That cannot be allowed to happen."

The pair nodded agreement.

He set the next date for them to meet in this place, in this their most sacred and secret place.

They began the sing.

Truck Trip

Stream and Lou had been relaxing for a number of days.

"O.K., partner!" announced Stream as she stormed, sorta, into the kitchen, large grey and white patterned towel wrapped around her hair. She was wearing her favorite, and much worn, yellow robe.

Lou looked over at her, returned to the large cast iron skillet sizzling on the stove, and gave the scrambled eggs, laid by real hens, another stir.

"Almost done," he replied. "Pour the coffee."

He was wearing the pajamas that Stream had given him, the top fastened by the lowest button. Various Disney characters capered here and there on his garb.

Banging two thick white mugs loudly on the kitchen table, she filled them, sat, took a sip, and pushed the other across the table toward his place setting. And looked at what she could see of him made visible through the large gap of his mostly unfastened pajama top.

What did he do to collect so many scars.

Lou turned from the stove, reached out and dumped a large heap of the scrambled eggs onto her plate, then the remaining eggs on his, turned back, switched skillets, and scooped and dumped a large mound of hash browns next to her egg mountain, then some onto his plate, replaced the skillet on the stove, burner turned off, and handed over a basket of toast, and a platter of bacon cooked to a crisp stage.

She smiled at him as he sat.

"Real food," stated Lou, spreading raspberry jam on his piece of toast.

She shrugged. "Yep." And bit the piece of bacon she held by two fingers.

For a short while they ate in silence and enjoyed the quiet of early morning as the sun streamed through the kitchen windows and lit up the walls.

"Now what?" Lou took a sip from his coffee.

"Lots of driving."

"Oh?"

"Uh huh."

As they cleaned things, she added, "Camping, truck camping, real luxury camping."

"Sure."

Finished with their chores, both headed to their bedrooms to dress in suitable clothes.

Then Stream walked ahead of him to the appropriate room, the one where all the camping gear, as they might need for various trips, was stored. She began to point.

"Tent, coolers, propane stove, propane bottles, lantern, folding chairs and table, inflatable mattresses, sleeping bags, that box of dishes, cooking gear, and towels. I'll get the food boxes loaded."

She laughed, a happy laugh. "On the way out of town we can get salad stuff, ice, and real meat."

Lou began to cart everything out to her truck and to stow it all in the back in a number of dust proof containers. She had said "that one of these days" she would get a lid for the back of her rig.

Organizing everything took some time, but eventually they were done and on the road, first stopping for the necessary items some of which went into the large cooler along with blocks of ice, then heading out of town. Soon they were traveling on a not too far from town road that slowly turned into less and less of one.

A number of hours later, Stream waggled one hand at their surrounding. "Where we are going there is lots of open space. Not too many folk, damn few actually. Tight knit groups, small settlements, isolated, by choice, more or less."

Late in the afternoon, Stream slowed up from the not very fast miles per hour, controlled by the condition of the road, the road being what it was, dirt, more or less paved, more or less smooth, and drove off the road into the totally barren looking openness, parked, and shut off the truck.

She jumped down and told him as he walked around to join her, "We could camp on the road with as little traffic as there is out here, but one never knows, someone might decided to take a drive at night."

Walking to the rear of the truck, she lowered the

tail gate, and began to haul out stuff.

As she began to unfold and set up the table and chairs, she looked at Lou. "I don't think that we will require the tent. I just brought it in case. I will make dinner and we can enjoy the open silence out here while we eat."

Stream made dinner and served. It was, for their usual camping style, rather elegant, sitting at a table in chairs, having dinner and then dessert.

As they relaxed after all that, Lou reached over a gently tapped her coffee cup with his and smiled. "This is what civilized camping was really like back in the early explorer days by as was done by the very wealthy. All that is missing is our numba one servant to fetch and carry. And maybe candles on the table."

She laughed, a happy, relaxed sound.

"Don't get spoiled, partner. I rarely ever camp this way." She sighed dramatically. "But we will just have to suffer our way along for the next bunch of days."

"Bunch of days?"

"Yep."

"Oh."

"We will get to the first spot in, um, about two, three days. The road is sorta marginal most of the way so the drive will be slow."

Lou nodded and looked up at the sky. "We ought," he suggested, "to be able to get two or three games in before it gets too dark." He waggled one hand loosely at her. "After we clean up, of course."

They cleaned dishes, pots, and whatever else needed cleaning, then they managed to play two games of cribbage before it got too dark. Each won one game.

"We could turn on a lantern," suggested Stream.

"Nope. Let's just sit, stare at all those stars, and listen to the quiet all around us."

"Right, partner," replied Stream.

He was really losing a lot of his urban world view.

They sat and did. Just relaxing and recuperating from their last trip surrounded by night and open space, sipping some nice red wine.

Early in the morning, they stood, coffee cups steaming soft curls upward, and watched the sun, soon to warm up the environment, rise over the far horizon.

Lou set his cup on the table and rapidly prepared breakfast.

It was another casual meal. There was no hurry. They would get to where they were going when they got there.

Lou nodded to himself.

All in all this was a different trip than many of the past ones they had made.

Stream heaved the tail gate of the truck up as soon as Lou had shoved in their packed camping gear.

And they were on their way, slowly traveling down a narrow, poorly maintained road.

"Stream?" asked Lou.

"What?"

"We just visiting?"

"Sorta. The boss had been hearing things and suggested that we ought to go forth and do this. I think that this is a kind of preliminary information gathering trip."

"Sure."

Three slow, relaxed days later they arrived.

Round Tom Anders stood looking out his office window.

It was a small office with the usual clutter one would expect to find in such an office.

One, old, somewhat battered, wooden desk, an in/out basket perched on one corner of the desk, at the moment empty of documents. The chair, an equally old and battered wooden swivel chair, stood just behind him. There were three wooden chairs with round somewhat comfortable backs, sitting here and there. Against one wall stood three, four-drawer filing cabinets with as small table , also against the wall, a coffee maker on top of it, plunged into a handy outlet.

Some weeks ago the plaza had been swarming with folk, venders and booths selling food and all manners of things. It had been the usual celebration of the village's settling.

He spun his wooden swivel chair around and dropped into it, propping his arms on the desk top.

Then he leaned back, the springs in the chair

making their usual complaint, and watched the door. He had seen her park and head in his direction with some guy.

So what is she up to this time? Way out here?

He waited. And waited.

A vague shape on the other side of the frosted glass rapped gently on that glass.

"Come on in!"

The pair did.

"Heya, Stream." He waggled one hand at the chairs.

"Round Tom," she stated as she sat. "This is my partner, Lou."

Round Tom nodded, eyes carefully checked her partner and wondered about whatever she had been doing since the last time she had visited and what is she was doing with a partner like that guy sitting there looking all relaxed. He looked to Round Tom like a person that was as tough and capable as anyone Round Tom had ever met before.

"Coffee?" he asked them.

They both nodded.

So he stood, poured three thick walled, white porcelain mugs full from his always full coffee maker, handed one to each, and sat and took a sip from his mug.

Stream did the same and smiled across the desk. "As good as ever."

"You've come aways."

"Yep." She nodded. "Tell us about that child that went missing."

He nodded, now really wondering what she was up to this time, and told her, in detail.

Round Tom looked at his coffee cup. It was empty. Then he looked at them.

"Staying? Overnight?"

Stream nodded. "Yep."

"Good! Then I will buy lunch. You can stay at my place." He stood. "Maize will be happy to cook a large meal."

Stream and Lou stood. She stared to Round Tom.

"Maize? . . . Round?"

Round Tom ducked his head and stepped from behind the desk.

"Yep." He grinned at her.

"I saw you park and phoned and told her that you would be staying overnight."

Stream's frown deepened.

"I've know Maize," explained Round Tom, "since grade school."

He ducked his head again and opened the door.

"We have the same birthdays. And as you know, her husband has been dead for a number of years, ummmm, now."

Stream gave Round a friendly thump on his shoulder. "Let's go eat lunch. I'll buy the beverages for dinner. Same place to have lunch, same stuff?"

"Yep. Ah, Maize likes it. As well."

"Soooo," said Stream as they walked across the plaza toward lunch, "what else, if anything, has happened here since my last visit?"

"Wellllll," began Round, "old Jimmy Jane was causing . . . "

Finally, they were all relaxing in Round Tom's living room. Several doors led into other areas of the sprawling ranch style house. Lunch had been a slow process of eating interspersed with conversation. Then they had relocated to here.

Dinner, was good food, well prepared, with fine beverages of several sorts, and more conversation mainly revolving around the local culture and customs, and some of the more colorful residents whose behavior was always a topic of discussion for the local population. All in all, it was a grand meal. It had been very relaxing, and all talked late into the evening.

But morning came, as it always does, with clear blue skies and a sun intent upon warming everything.

Stream and Lou and their hosts were not too quick to crawl from their beds and greet the new day. But they eventually did.

After a hardy breakfast, Round Tom and Maize stood on the front deck and waved goodbye as Stream headed her truck up the road to the main route through this mostly open and uninhabited space.

Lou and Stream sipped Maize's dark coffee from

travel cups, now and then, as she drove toward the far horizon.

Lou set his cup in the holder on the dash, stretched as much as their space would allow, and grunted, a soft sound.

"What?"

"Well," he began.

"What?"

"Do you know everybody?"

"Nope."

"Oh?"

"I have just traveled, ahh, widely, ummm, for various reasons. That's all."

"Sure." He nodded and retrieved his coffee container and took another sip.

They drove on, neither feeling it necessary to fill in the silence with idle talk.

Sometime around noon, some time around mid-day, more or less, Stream drove off the road and parked.

"Lunch time," she announced as she dropped to the ground. "I am going to walk out there aways and you, good fellow that you are, are going to unload stuff for lunch and keep your eyes focused on that chore."

After she returned, they opened the various coolers, made sandwiches, sat on the down tail gate, and ate the prepared lunch.

Lou wagged his half-eaten sandwich at their surroundings. "Pretty open."

"Yep." She took a big bite from her sandwich, ham, turkey, sliced tomatoes. "Low population density."

"Sure." Lou swallowed and made another sandwich.

So did Stream.

They put everything back, and shut the tail gate.

The followed the same routine for the next several days of their travel.

Finally, at noon, sorta noon, they parked off the road, ate sandwiches, and looked out into vast open space.

Stream pointed, "Couple of hours that way there is a nice spot to camp. We will just take it easy. From that spot I will phone the local sheriff and tell him that we will see him in the morning."

And, as she had said, two hours later, sorta, the pulled off the road and camped. Stream made her phone call.

They played a few games of cribbage before and after dinner and then did what she had suggested. They took it easy.

Lou smiled out at their surroundings and thought that this was the most continuous relaxing that he had ever done.

He lurched up from his large easy chair, set the book that he had been reading on the handy table next to his chair, lumbered toward the noisy instrument.

The phone rang.

Again.

The brass name plate over his left pocket told all who looked that this person was "Officer Rona MacKenzie."

Rona, pronounced locally as Ro Nah, not Ron Ah as the few strangers who read his bronze name tag said his name.

Rona MacKenzie yanked up the phone in a strangle hold. Far back in the dim distant past a large Scotsman had arrived, survived the encounter with the local tribe and had taken a wife, hence his family name.

"Uh?" he grumbled into the phone.

Rona always answered the phone that way. As it was normal and usual, whoever local called weren't put off by his response, not at all. The time of day had nothing to with his response.

His thick leather belt supported a very large holster and large revolver. It kinna reinforced the name plate statement. He had started reading and forgot to take it off.

"See you then," he said.

Yanking off that belt hung with his gun and other things, he dropped it on the small table, sat down and snatched up his book.

At the appropriate time in the morning, he climbed into his large and never washed truck and headed for town, as everyone called this small disordered cluster of houses, and aimed for the one where Slim Jem Halaban lived.

From his place, one of the few sorta isolated places, to her place was about a ten minute drive if one drove at the usual rate of speed around here, not too fast, not too slow. Slim Jem claimed a long distance ancestor had created the family name after some sort of argument with a relative.

Rona was sure that Slim Jem will cook up some beer pancakes for them and their visitors.

He parked in front of her house, noting that the visitors hadn't arrived yet, climbed down, walked over and gave the door a soft rap with one knuckle and pushed it open.

"IN!" called a loud voice as he stepped inside and closed the door. It was Slim Jem's usual greeting.

After explaining why he was here, Slim Jem headed into her kitchen and began to make breakfast for everyone. Today it was not going to be an ordinary breakfast but one of her special breakfasts.

Rona stood, walked into the kitchen, and back again, carrying a stack of heavy duty thick white plates and a fistful of knives and forks and set the table in the living room. Her kitchen wasn't large enough for that.

Rona stood by one of the large windows and watched a large and dirty truck approaching.

Well, here she comes. Wonder what she is up to this time.

As the pair walked toward the door, he walked over and opened it.

"Stream," he said by way of greeting, his eyes checking out her companion.

"Rona," she said, pronouncing his name correctly, "this is Lou, my partner."

Rona nodded and closed the door after they entered.

They sat at the table.

"Pretty soon," called Slim Jem from the kitchen.

Rona poured their cups full from the coffee container on the table and waited.

Slim Jem walked from the kitchen holding several large platters which she thumped onto the table.

"That ought to do it," she stated, smiling warmly at Rona. "Stream."

"Looks good," observed Stream. "This is Lou, my partner."

"Eat," said Slim Jem.

While everyone was hard at work consuming pancakes and bacon, the front door banged open and Charity Jane and her grandmother entered.

The grandmother thumped into the house, a thick hiking stick keeping time on the floor with her steps.

THUMP!

THUMP!

THUMP!

Rona handed a plate, a knife and a fork, and

chairs to each of them.

Lou looked from person to person. He felt like a midget in this company. It appeared that everyone here all came in a very large size.

Grandmother slowly cut precise pieces from her pancakes and bacon strips. Then she slowly chewed each piece.

There were times when Rona was convinced that much of what she did was theater. He thought that now. But he knew better than say anything like that.

Grandmother finally shoved the plate towards the middle of the table.

"Um ah," she grunted.

She looked at Stream.

"That one," she stated clearly, "was a Nightwalker. He thought to gain dark power from the bones of a young child."

She smiled at Slim Jem and grunted, "Good breakfast, Tall Beauty."

She lurched to her feet, turned away and headed for the front door, walking staff thumping loudly on the wooden floor, waggling one arm at Charity Jane. The pair left the house, closing the door behind them.

Stream looked at Rona. "Who? One?"

Rona told them.

Ranching

Charles Stands had grown up in what many of the folk who lived in what they called a civilized setting would view as a rather desolate land. He didn't see it that way at all. He had seen it as a place to raise cattle, a place with far horizons.

It had taken a number of years of work and massive determination to make his idea came true. Now he owned, or leased, a very large piece of land upon which his cattle wandered. In this region it took a lot of acres, given the local vegetation, to raise the number of cattle that he raised successfully.

Today, on this day, he stood with his foreman alongside one of the many corrals scattered all over his vast holdings.

Charles Stands was the name listed on all the deeds, contracts, and other legal documents that were required for his business to be in business.

He was tall. It came from his mother's side of the family. He was sorta slender. It came from his father's side of the family along with light blue eyes and dark brown, sorta light dark brown, hair color.

When he was growing up he was comfortable by nature and by choice to being by himself. So, he was named by his grandmother, Stands Alone. His father called him Tomas regardless of local customs.

When he was a grown man and had started on his endeavor he called himself Charles Stands and made the name legal for all purposes having to do with paperwork and the other aspects of the world he had one foot planted in.

The friends he grew up with usually called him Tomas. Most of his relatives on his mother's side of the extended kin called him Stands Alone. He answered to it all.

Today, on this day, he stood next to one of his many corrals, watching the light breeze ruffle its way across the open space around this place.

He looked at the corral and frowned.

Next to the railing stood a rather small man, standing almost on his tip toes. His hands were tied behind his back. A noose around his neck held him in his strange vertical posture.

The noose rope ran over the top rail and was tied off to the saddle horn of a well trained horse who stood quietly inside the corral waiting for Charles to say something.

"Tow Mas," said Gather Many Horses in his normal soft voice, "I do not think that you should do this thing."

"Uh ah?"

Off to one side of the two men stood six others watching them, all range riders and one very young male child, seven years old. The child, a son of the rider with a heavy squint, had been working at this corral.

"Useta hang rustlers," stated Charles. "This is worse."

"It is so," agreed Gather Many Horses, then he cleared his throat.

"Eh?"

"That one will speak to me."

Charles stared into the distance and thought about it.

Gather Many Horses waited, as patient as patient can be.

The silence wrapped around them all as Charles thought.

Then he sighed, a long, soft sigh. And nodded.

Gather Many Horses walked over to the small man, slipped the nose free, grabbed him by the front of his upper garment and dragged him into the small shed attached to the corral.

It was the end of their work day as Stream drove down her street and parked the big truck.

"That's interesting," observed Lou.

A horse stood quietly in front of the closed and locked gate to Stream's house. Sitting on the street, leaning back against the gate, sitting apparently quite comfortable there, were a man and a very young child. They were both quite dusty looking as if they had ridden a long distance just to come and sit in front of her gate.

Stream jumped down from her rig and walked over to them as they stood.

"Heya, Squints Alot," she greeted the pair.

Nudging, gently, the horse to one side, she unlocked the gate and pulled it open.

"Come in. I'll get something to eat and drink." She urged her guests inside and tugged the horse along into the interior space.

She waggled her free hand at Lou.

He slid across the front seat and slowly drove the truck after them. Then he jumped down and closed and locked the gate.

He nodded to himself.

Things always seemed to happen around her.

In the living room, Stream yanked a small Navajo rug from the back of the large couch and spread it on the floor and hurried into the kitchen. Soon she had a number of dishes and platters covered with food set on the rug as well as glasses and jugs of water and juice.

She sat, served everyone and waited quietly while everyone ate, drank, and relaxed.

When she was satisfied that all were done she cleared everything away, returned, sat, and waited.

Squints Alot cleared his throat.

"Ummm?" said Stream.

Lou sat there, a silent observer.

What was going on, this time?

Squints Alot unbuttoned his shirt, reached inside and pulled out a number of pieces of paper folded into a tight package. He handed it to her.

"Stands Alone sends this." He nodded. "You will know what to do."

He stood as did the very young boy. The man buttoned his shirt, and nodded at Stream.

"You have provisions?" she asked them.

"Eh ah. Enough."

Stream walked them out to the parking space, unlocked and pushed the gate open. She watched them ride slowly out, down the street, and out into the vast open space not too far away.

Closing and locking the gate, she returned to the living room.

Lou now sat in one of the chairs, filled coffee cup in hand.

As she sat in the couch, she said by way of explanation, "Stands Alone, Charles Stands, is a rancher with a very large cattle spread way, way out there. Friends and relatives work on it. Something very not good happened out there."

She unfolded the papers and looked up. "How about bringing me a big cup of coffee."

"Sure."

Lou headed for the kitchen as Stream began to read.

Home Again

After a leisurely breakfast, Stream and Lou strolled into her office, checked the large "mail box" next to the door just inside the room. It was empty, for once.

Stream spun around, stepped into the door, and looked back over her shoulder.

"Work on something, Lou. I am going to go and talk with the boss."

She strode down the hall and around the far corner.

Lou sat at one of the work tables and turned on the computer. While it worked its way into a state of waiting to do business, he wondered again.

Now what is she up to?

Then he began to read the conclusion of the small report they had been working on. And lost track of time as he checked data against conclusion.

She banged into the office, jolted him from his deep concentration as she grabbed her jacket from the hanger.

"Let's go, partner! We have a cop to talk to."

He swivelled around and stared at her.

"Ummm?"

She pointed at the computer display. "That can wait!"

"Sure."

Lou waggled his mouse, and clicked.

Everything shut down.

He stood, grabbed his jacket draped over the back of his chair, and pulled it on.

They headed down the hall toward the appropriate parking lot.

Some time later, across town, Stream parked in an open slot next to the architecturally imposing headquarters of the city police.

She led Lou to a side door, down a hall, and then up a flight of stairs and then another flight and down the hall. She stopped in front of a door, opened it, and walked in.

It was a very large office occupied by a single individual who looked up and smiled at her.

"Matias Meredith," she stated, "this is Lou, my partner. Talk to us!"

He laughed, a very relaxed sound that said that he wasn't surprised by her, and pointed at some very comfortable chairs. Then he pressed a button, one of the many on a panel at the left edge of his desk.

So from where did Stream get a partner like this guy?

"Coffee for three, please. Just black all around."

Leaning back in his chair, he smiled at them as they sat.

"What, exactly, would you like to talk about?"

Stream nodded. "Tell you in a moment."

The door opened and a very large man carried in

a tray holding three large steaming mugs. He set the tray on the desk top, the very clean desk top.

"Thanks," said Matias.

The man nodded, turned, and left.

After all had taken a sip or two and waited the appropriate amount of time, Stream cleared her throat.

"Uh huh?" replied Matias.

"Not too long ago," began Stream, "Lou and I took a trip out into the way out there."

Matias nodded.

"We visited with Round Tom and Rona MacKenzie. And this is what we learned." She told him in detail. "Then, after we returned, we heard from Charles Stands, and this is what those folk told us." It was another detailed exposition.

When she finished her talk and her coffee, Matias leaned back in his chair, holding his mug. "Most interesting."

Stream smiled at him.

"So, tell us about your three cases."

"Certainly."

Matias pushed the same button again and waited until the same large man entered and took the tray and coffee mugs away.

"Rather puzzling cases," he began. "But all having a certain similarity."

Then he told them everything that he saw and that he thought. He leaned back in his chair.

"So you see, we do not really know much, but it does seem to lead into other areas not inside my jurisdiction, or perhaps even that of the state folks."

He smiled at her. "What do you think?"

She stood.

"I think that I have to go talk with someone who might have a good idea about all this."

Matias nodded.

"You will let me know?"

"Sure."

She spun and headed for the door as Lou stood.

"Let's go."

After that door slowly closed, Matias stared at it for some time.

Who really was that fellow with Stream? He certainly wasn't some paper pushing flunky that she was leading around. That was for sure.

He leaned back in his chair, tapped a button, and listened to the dialing noise that his speaker phone emitted.

"Yes?"

"Hello, boss. You want to tell me what she is up to this time?"

The boss laughed, and did.

She hurried from the building and toward her truck.

As soon as he jumped in, she started down the street, just a wee bit over the legal limit.

"My place first. We'll load all our camping gear then go to your place. Take only rugged and heavy duty clothes and boots."

Once they were inside her house, she led him to the correct room and began to point out at the things to take.

"Hurry, Lou, hurry."

She dashed down the hall to the kitchen, picked the phone and hit a button.

"Hi, boss. I'll be gone for some unknown amount of time. Will explain when I return."

She hurried away and back again holding a number of empty boxes and began to stuff the food into them.

Lou had hurried, as suggested, and had loaded all their gear in her truck.

Now they were headed across town to gather up some of his belongings. As they left her place, Lou looked back at her open gate.

"Don't worry about it," she said. "It will be taken care of."

"Ummm?"

"What?"

"Is going on?" she stated, finishing his question for him.

"Yep."

"We're heading up to the Pacific Northwest to where my parents live and where I grew up. We'll just camp here and there along the way whenever we feel like it."

"What's the rush?"

"None."

"Oh?"

"Just felt like it." She laughed. "Sorta."

"Um."

He sighed very quietly to himself.

They finally arrived at her parent's place in the late dusk of a summer day. The last portion of the drive was slower as the long dirt mountain road wandered through dense forest until they it crossed a large open meadow surrounded by very tall pine and other species of the local area. She parked next to the house sitting at the far edge of that meadow.

A woman was sitting on the swing on the front porch, slowly rocking back and forth.

She stopped, stood, and came down the wooden stairs.

Her skin was a soft brown, her eyes black as her hair.

"Welcome home, daughter," she said as she hugged her.

Once she was released, Stream told her, "This is my partner, Lou. Partner at work. You've already met him, remember?"

Her mother laughed.

Of course she remembered. Someone like him would be remembered by those who truly saw him.

"Inside you two, my husband is just finishing dinner and is right now putting it on the table. You can probably use a good meal after your trip."

As Lou trailed them inside the house he felt his mouth began to salivate as the odors of dinner assaulted his nostrils.

"Smells really, really good." He felt extremely hungry.

Stream's mother pointed. "You may wash in there, if you wish."

Lou headed in the correct direction, washed his hands and face, then followed the sounds of soft conversation and the clattering of dinner plates being set in place.

A tall, slim man smiled at him and indicated a chair at the table. "Sit here, Lou."

And as soon as the others sat in their places, he said, "Help yourself to whatever is close and then pass it to your left." He took a large scoop of mashed potatoes and handed the bowl to Stream, who sat to his left. Then he ladled gravy over his serving and set that bowl in front of her.

Lou dragged the platter closer to his plate.

"Turkey and German sausage," explained her father. "Take whatever you wish. I will have both."

The plates were large but soon filled with some of everything on the table.

The conversation, and the questions, were as gentle as the parent's voices.

Once the dessert was demolished, a smooth as silk cheese cake, they moved to the living room where her father filled tall glasses with a light brown liquid.

"Made locally. Some folks got licensed to make

whiskey."

He took a swallow and then looked at Stream.

"So, daughter. Why are you here? I can tell that this is not just a social call, a long past due social call."

She shook her head.

Stream stared at them. "You were expecting me?"

"It is so," replied her mother.

"How did you know?" whispered Stream.

Her father nodded at his wife.

"The wolves told me," she stated.

She pointed toward the outside. "The three packs that have drifted into this area from the Montana and Wyoming areas over the years."

"The . . . wolves . . . told . . . you?"

"Most so," replied her mother. "They have been singing for the past three nights."

She took a swallow from her glass.

"Even the song dogs, who fear the wolves, came close enough to sing the same message."

"Wolves and coyotes again?" stated Stream.

"It is so."

She pointed. "When the moon is there, we will sit on the porch swing and you will tell me everything."

Stream nodded.

Dark eyes watched her face carefully and turned to Lou.

"You are looking fine and well, warrior."

Lou blinked and took a sip from his glass.

Her mother nodded at him and looked at Stream.

"Now we will speak of small town happenings and things like that."

And soon, Stream sat on the porch in the swing with her mother while her father "entertained" Lou in the kitchen. Stream could tell that her father was even more curious about this fella that she had dragged home again than he had been the last time she had done that.

Her mother slowly pushed the swing back and forth.

"You know, talented daughter, that my ancestors have been around for a long, long time."

Stream nodded. "American Indian."

Her mother laughed. "Truly a nonsense term. We are not American anything. For all those thousands of years we were Indians. Even though we were murdered into submission, the nonsense P.C. terms used today signify nothing except gross ignorance on the part of the folk who use them and who fail to recognize that we are the First People."

She patted her daughter's thigh.

"We are a different bunch than all those late comers. We see things differently, we think about things differently, and we do things differently."

"It is why I have come."

"Um hum."

"I need some cultural data and help in understanding."

"Ah hum. About what? Something you are involved in?"

Stream nodded and slowly, carefully, related everything that she had learned, been told, about the kidnappings and attempted kidnappings in her local area. Then she described the events she had learned about in the land way out beyond.

Lou drifted quietly onto the porch and sat on a step to listen.

"Soooo," hissed her mother when Stream had finished. "The grandmother called that one a Nightwalker?"

"She did."

"Dark things, dark thoughts."

"What are?"

"Some of the people call them Shape Shifters. Some of the people call them Skin Changers."

Stream nodded.

"They are folk who believe that they can do that. They are a hidden folk, hidden from the people they live around. To be found out for that is to die!"

"Why?" asked Lou.

"There are always folk," explained Stream's mother, "who believe in the dark things, the dark mysteries, in the dark powers, in many cultures. Among the people those are the labels for those kind of folk. They believe if they perform certain horrible things that they will gain special powers, powers to make them above those they live among."

"There is a difference between folk who believe and folk who act on those beliefs," stated Stream.

Her mother reached over and took one of

Stream's hands in hers. "Hard to find, the very secretive folk, those who act."

She stared into somewhere else for a period of time and then sighed loudly.

"Soft word," she whispered, "has come. It says that a number of those who believe in dark things have come together to do dark actions. Everything that you told says that this is so."

"Stream daughter you must talk with those who wander the great open spaces and ask them what they have seen and smelled. Even the most careful folk cannot hide from those who see further, whose senses know when a person is around."

Stream stared at her.

"And if I find this out?"

"Those dark ones must die! Talk with Cohan first."

Lou jerked upright from his comfortable slump

Stream's mother laughed softly at his reaction. Then she patted the hand that she held.

"Stay some days here. It will be good. Good for you. Good for us."

Stream looked at Lou.

"Sure," he said.

It sounded like a good idea.

Well, That Is Interesting

After leaving Stream's parent's place, they traveled towards home. Very leisurely they traveled.

They camped often, at times driving less than a day from camping place to camping place, from one interesting spot to the next interesting spot.

No rush, no bother. Just relaxing.

If there were trails to hike, they hiked.

If there were scenic features to view, they did that.

Eventually they arrived.

Lou jumped from the truck and swung open the large outside door in the wall, waited for her to drive in, then closed and latched the gate.

The next few days were spent cleaning and packing away the camping gear so it would be ready to be used the next time.

In-between those and other chores, they wandered the surrounding neighborhood, visiting here and there, purchasing this or that thing to eat, and loafing.

Then it was time to go back to work.

So they did.

Stream parked in one of the secure parking areas. They passed through security, wandered down the hall, and around a corner to Stream's office.

Two small boxes stuffed with documents sat on top of her desk. The attached note told them that this project was not one in a hurry.

Stream read another note and looked at Lou.

"Um hum," she said.

"What?" He hung his coat on one of the hooks. This time.

"From the boss. It says that as soon as we get in you should go and see him in his office.

"Ermmm?"

"I have no idea," she murmured.

He shrugged. "Oh well." He stopped in the open door, holding the door and turned toward her. "Ahhhh, which way?"

Stream smiled. "Down the hall to your left. Turn at the intersection to your right. His door is at the far end. Can't miss it."

He nodded, stepped into the hall, releasing the door, and turned to his left, and strolled casually towards his destination.

He wandered along the hall somewhat puzzled.

What was going on this time. As far as he could tell, they hadn't upset any organization. Yet. Mostly all they had been doing, so far, was gathering information on a very puzzling series of events.

He gave a mental shrug, strolled around the corner, to the right, and down the very long hall.

At the appropriate door, the only one at the very

end of the hall, he stopped. He took a deep breath, slowly exhaled, relaxed, and pushed the door open and walked in.

It was a large room, with a moderately sized desk, one phone, a computer terminal, and a few chairs in front of the desk.

The boss smiled at him. "Sit anywhere, Lou."

Lou picked the most comfortable looking of the chairs and sat.

The boss poured two cups of coffee from a container on his desk and held one toward Lou.

After each had taken a sip or two, the boss nodded, mostly to himself.

"It appears to me," he began, "that you and Stream have developed into a very impressive team." He laughed. "If you can call two people a team, that is."

He held up one hand to stop any comments that Lou might be about to make.

"I am impressed. Really, I am. We have gone through a fairly large number of people, male and female, trying to find someone that could work with her and, ahhhhh, survive. She fired them for various reasons."

The boss refilled his cup.

"As you obviously now know, she has a rather, ummm, unorthodox approach to doing her job as well as her, ermmmm, need for recreation as well as having some interesting, also unorthodox, acquaintances."

Lou nodded. Slowly.

So where was all this conversation going?

"You," stated the boss with emphasis, "were my very own, ha, unorthodox choice for her partner. And, as I said, I think, I am very, very happy how you two have worked so well together. Not just well, but very creative, very professional, very effective."

Lou nodded again.

"You met her parents?"

Lou nodded a third time.

Answers weren't really required.

"Soooo, you can see where her looks come from, from her mother's side from ancestors that stretch back into unknown history. She has also inherited an ability to always know where she is in the environment. She has sense of where she is and where she wants to go. Her father can do this. No maps. No compass. Just that very rare ability. Both of them have a strong need to be outside. You surely know that by now."

The boss leaned back in this chair and took a studied look at Lou.

Who sat and waited. Relaxed.

The boss laughed.

And sat up. "No wonder! You are her other half. You are the balance." He swallowed some coffee and frowned, just a wee bit. "Of course, you are also her most lethal half as well. That was the reason we hired you. But, now, you have become ever so much more in your activities than that, ever so much more."

The boss sat up and leaned toward Lou.

"I talked with her parents a long time ago when I was deciding whether I should hire her or not. I had heard, through my usual grapevine, about this very bright young woman. I heard that this talented individual irritated the bureaucratic structures where she worked by operating outside those structures and producing results faster than that structure could. So, as you can imagine, vested interests saw she moved on to some other job. I am sure you are now very familiar with her approach to her work and you do function quite well with it. Now, I am going to tell you all about your partner. Perhaps, someday, when you feel like it, you will tell her all about yourself."

The boss leaned back, took a sip from his ever-filled coffee cup, and began.

Once Again Cohan

Lou strolled slowly down the hall, deep in thought.

So she is just more amazing than he knew or had seen.

He laughed, a not quite audible laugh. And shrugged.

The boss certainly knew a lot about Stream's intellectual abilities and her upbringing. But, my oh my, would he be surprised at some of her other unique talents. Well, that was up to her to decide who knew about this or that. It wasn't his business to be blabbing about anything to anyone about any aspect of his partner.

He shrugged again.

His thoughts had nothing to do with his "job," not at all. It had to do with his ever developing relationship with her.

After all, he had been hired to protect her, just that and nothing more. That was no longer merely his occupation. It has become a personal, a very, very personal thing to do.

He stopped outside their office and peered through the glass door at her, totally engrossed in working on one of their many reports.

She smiled and looked up

Damn! How does she do that.

He shoved the door open and walked in.

"Just in time!" She laughed. "Not really."

She stood, snatched her coat from a hook on the wall.

"For?" he asked.

She headed for the door.

"We're off to visit our mystical map maker, the wizard of ambiguous statements, and the creator of lethal alcoholic beverages."

He followed her down the hall after snatching his coat from the hook on the wall.

"Cohan?"

"Right-o-rooney." She giggled, waved at the security folk, and hurtled outside and over to her very large, quite dusty, truck.

He climbed into the right hand seat, fastened his seat belt, and slammed the door shut.

"Right-o-rooney?"

"Just felt like it."

The truck drifted into the street and purred along with the traffic headed across town.

Lou thought that its original color probably had been a dark brown.

Far across town, in an area of rather modest looking houses that had lots of open space between them, Stream pulled into a driveway and parked in front of one, nicely painted, white with pale blue trim around the door and windows.

Lou looked at it. And nodded, looks the same as their last visit.

She strode up to the front door and tried the knob.

"Locked!"

Stream kicked the bottom of the door with a boot tip.

"OPEN UP!"

"Meow, meow, meow," purred a voice from the speaker mounted above the door.

"Co . . . han," she snarled as she kicked the door four more times, each harder than the last.

"COHAN, OPEN THE DAMN DOOR!"

Lou heard several electric locks pop and unlatch.

Stream opened the door and stepped inside the short hall, shutting the door behind Lou as he entered.

The locks relatched.

"Ahhhhhh," said the voice of someone out of sight, "we are being visited once again by the ever so delightful Stream with her stud side-kick. Do come in."

Lou looked at her. She shrugged. It was just Cohan being Cohan.

And led him into a large windowless room, and turned to the right.

A very large man sat comfortably slouched in a short plush couch.

Stream and Lou sat in the only two chairs.

Cohan rose to his feet, a very careful, choreographic production of standing up.

"I," stated Cohan, "in spite of the early hour, am going to have a wee bit of this or that." He smiled at them. "Actually more than a mere wee bit. Would you like something? Coffee? Tea? Other?"

"Coffee," stated Stream. "For two. Black."

"Most certainly." Cohan flowed from the room, all graceful movement.

He returned, bearing a very large tray which held a coffee container, two large cups, and a bottle of some liquid that glittered in the light.

He set the coffee container on a small table between Stream and Lou, handed each of them a cup, and took the bottle in one hand and sailed the tray to one side where it landed on the middle cushion of the large couch.

Settling in his short couch, Cohan took a long pull from his bottle, opened in his kitchen. He didn't bother with a glass.

He held out the bottle and sloshed the contents back and forth.

"RUM, BY GUM! The drink of Pirates and that sort of ilk. Yo, ho, ho, ho, etc."

He took another swallow, set the bottle on the floor beside his chair, and leaned toward Stream.

His eyes swivelled to Lou, his gaze seemed to bore into Lou's eyes.

"She is a great treasure, as you know, our Stream. She is one that must be protected, one that must be allowed to do all that she has chosen to do. Gird your loins, strong one. Take up your weapons, you will have terrible and bloody work to do once again." This was spoken in a very rolling Shakespearian tone of voice, a very regal tone of voice.

Stream tried not to blush.

Cohan winked at her, leaned back, snatched up his bottle from the floor, and emptied it in one very long swallow. Then he smiled at her.

"So, how goes everything with you two?"

They sipped their coffee, watched Cohan walk into his kitchen and return with another bottle of something.

Lou and Cohan waited for Stream to start.

Finally she decided it was time to proceed, having noted the very subtle shift in Cohan's posture as he settled himself into a comfortable slouch. She checked Lou, who appeared completely relaxed, which she knew was not at all true, and nodded at Cohan.

"I need to get from you some very concrete answers."

Cohan winked at her.

She started to explain.

It took a long time.

Stream told him everything. She told him about every visit, every comment, everything. All about dirt and footprints, dead bodies, missing children, and on, and on, and on, and on.

Cohan sat statue still. He could have been dead. But he breathed slowly.

Then he stood and stretched.

He seemed to fill that part of the room.

"Tomorrow! Come back tomorrow!"

He headed for the kitchen, stopped, and turned.

He smiled a very broad smile at them.

"We'll have lunch."

He waggled on hand at them.

"See ya, pussy cat."

He disappeared into the rest of his house.

Stream stood, walked down the short hall and banged outside, down the short walkway to her truck.

Behind them they heard all the locks snap into place on the front door.

As she drove toward their office, she looked over at Lou.

"That went well, don't you think?"

"No idea."

"It did."

A number of blocks later, and a few turns, she parked.

"Let's have a leisurely lunch."

Lou looked. They had parked in front of a Chinese restaurant.

"Sure." He jumped down and started for the front door.

So, they had a very leisurely lunch.

They had lots of fluffy white rice to go with egg rolls with sweet and sour sauce, winter melon soup with chicken, egg Fu Yung, stir-fried shrimp with peas, chicken in plum sauce, lots of green tea sipped from tiny cups, and honey walnuts for dessert. All the servings were on the small side. Stream had stressed that to the waiter.

So, it was a very leisurely lunch of two hours or

so.

After paying the bill, they piled into her truck and headed off, relaxed, very relaxed.

She turned a corner and turned again.

"This day is pretty much shot," she stated. "Let's head home and take it easy."

"Sure."

"I've got a bottle of a nice white wine in the frig. It is just the thing to have after that meal."

Lou laughed. "Sounds good to me."

As they sat in the larger of the two couches, taking a sip now and then, Lou laughed.

"What?"

"Partner," he said.

"What?"

"This is the most amazing job that I ever have had."

"Oh?"

"Yep."

"So?" she prompted.

"Let's see," he stated in a very academic tone of voice and presentation.

"Leisurely meals at the drop of hat, so to speak."

"Ummm."

"Camping, here, there, and everywhere, when ever."

"Umm huh."

"Living, off and on, with a very talented and traffic stopping babe, also so to speak."

"Huh uh."

"Meeting and greeting the local wild canines."

She reached over and refilled his glass, then her's.

"And so on and so forth," he concluded.

Stream took a sip.

"Doesn't seem all that amazing to me." She grinned at him, and added, "Other than my partner."

"Oh?" He looked over the rim of his glass at her. "Me?"

"Yep."

"Umm."

She cleared her throat.

"Uh huh. You are the most dangerous individual that I have ever met, all wrapped up in a quiet, very relaxed, non-threatening facade." She laughed. "It is very comforting. No matter what we are doing, I do feel quite safe."

"I am glad." He took a sip and nodded. Then he shrugged.

Well, I suppose that is alright.

And frowned.

"What?"

"When the boss hired me and told me why, I gave the job one month before I would quit. It sounded like so much nonsense. However . . . "

"What?"

"Wouldn't trade it for anything."

"Good. Me neither."

Lou twitched.

Stream stood, grabbed the empty bottle, and headed for the kitchen, and returned shortly with another one.

"Just a little red to finish the evening with."

She refilled her glass then his.

"Shiraz," she said.

They sat is quite comfort and sipped.

Sometime around the mid-point of that bottle, she slid sideways and leaned against him, forcing him to slide his arm up and around her shoulders.

"Umm?"

Now what is she doing?

"Like I said, very comforting."

"Sure."

It sounded good to him.

She leaned forward, set her glass on the table, slumped a little, and fell asleep nestled against him.

He sighed. "Oh well."

Lou emptied his glass, reached over the end of the couch and dropped it onto the rug, a very thick rug.

Then he took a deep breath and slowly let it out.

And fell asleep.

Stream's eyes popped open.

It was morning.

The smell of coffee drifted into the living room from the kitchen as did the trying to be quiet food preparing sounds. It all said to her that breakfast was on the way.

She sat up and stretched.

She was still on the couch. There was a pillow for her head and a cover from her bed still tucked around her.

She was still fully clothed minus her shoes which were lined up right at the edge of the couch.

"Fifteen minutes!" called Lou from the kitchen door.

She stood and headed down the hall to grab a quick shower and a change of clothes, carrying her blanket and pillow with her.

In more or less than the fifteen minutes, Stream stopped in the doorway to the kitchen and asked, "What's cooking?"

Lou spun from where he was working at the long counter and smiled at her.

"I was rummaging around in your refrigerator and saw a box of strawberries, so I checked here and there, and decided to make beer waffles."

"Which are?"

"Waffles with beer for liquid. You top them with some sour cream, sprinkle a little brown sugar over that, then heap sliced strawberries on top of everything."

He reached over, grabbed the coffee pot, and filled her cup at her place at the kitchen table.

"Ready when you are, Gridley," he said.

Stream took a sip of her coffee and nodded.

"Fire when ready," she ordered.

Stream pushed her plate away and held up her cup.

Lou filled it.

She took a sip and looked at him.

"Ready to see what Cohan has to say?"

"Sure." Lou emptied his cup and gathered everything that he could shove into the dish washer and turned it on.

"Ta dah!"

Off they went.

It was mostly a repeat performance.

Stream and Lou sat in the only two chairs.

Cohan rose to his feet, a very careful, choreographic production of standing up.

"I," stated Cohan, "in spite of the early hour, am going to have a wee bit of this or that." He smiled at them. "Actually more than a mere wee bit. Would you like something? Coffee? Tea? Other?"

"Coffee," stated Stream. "For two. Black."

"Most certainly." Cohan flowed from the room, all graceful movement. "You were supposed to come for lunch!" he said over his shoulder.

Cohan returned, bearing a very large tray which held a coffee container, two large cups, and a bottle of some liquid that glittered in the light.

He set the coffee container on a small table between Stream and Lou, handed each of them a cup, and took the bottle in one hand and sailed the tray to one side where it landed on the middle cushion of a large couch.

Settling in his short couch, Cohan took a long pull from his bottle, opened in his kitchen. He didn't bother with a glass.

He held out the bottle and sloshed the contents back and forth and shrugged at Stream.

She looked like she wasn't willing put up with a little humor at the moment.

Then he reached down past the side of his short couch and picked up a folder and handed it toward Stream.

"Names and addresses. This is a bunch of pretty nasty guys who want to believe in origin myths and seem to believe that they can affect things of the past for their benefit."

As she opened the folder and began to scan the pages, he added, "Careful, careful. They will kill you in a heartbeat."

He looked at Lou. "Understand?"

Lou nodded.

Any attempts at violence directed at Stream or himself would be terminal for whoever.

Cohan nodded. "When it is over tell me how your adventure went." He flashed her a quick smile. "Ah, if you survive."

"Sure," she said standing. "Let's go Lou." She nodded. "Thanks, Cohan."

He sighed. "Sometimes beliefs can be a real pain in the butt."

Stream headed outside to her truck.
As soon as Lou jumped in she headed off.
"We have gear to pack and plans to make."
"Sure."

Gathering

They entered her living room and headed for the kitchen.

Lou set the coffee maker to bubbling.

Stream nodded.

"I am going to sit in the living room and go over all the stuff that Cohan gave me. Gather all the gear that we will need for comfortable truck camping. I'll phone the boss and tell him that we are going to be gone for a number of days."

"Sure."

Lou headed down the hall to the room where they stowed all their camping gear. After pushing a box here and a box there, he began to carry items through the house and into the back of her truck.

Slowly the bed of the truck began to fill with all of the items they would be using for an extended trip of comfortable truck camping, camping in style.

After checking everything, just to make sure, he headed to his room for a few additional items that had nothing to do with camping in comfort. Although the things he selected did make him feel just a wee bit more comfortable.

Lou made breakfast, after which they packed the boxes with food for the trip, loaded them in the bed of the truck and then added two coolers.

Stream made a quick phone call to her house watchers, then one more call.

The phone rang.

The phone rang.

Rona MacKenzie, lurched into the living room and yanked up the phone in a strangle hold. He had been in the kitchen making something to eat.

"Uh?" he grumbled into the phone.

Rona always answered the phone that way so whoever called wasn't put off by his response, not at all. The time of day had nothing to with his response.

He grunted a few more times.

"I'll see you when you get here."

He hung up and walked outside.

Climbing into his large and never washed truck, he headed for town, as everyone called this small cluster of houses, and aimed for the one where Slim Jem Halaban lived.

Stream turned and looked at Lou.

"Ready?"

"Sure."

He headed outside and opened the large outside gate and waited for her to back out. Then he closed and locked the gate and climbed inside the truck.

On the way out of town they stopped at the

grocery store and bought the stuff that went into the coolers. After all, they were doing comfortable truck camping. That meant that they could treat themselves to all manner of items otherwise never considered when camping "way out there."

Soon, it always seemed soon to Lou, they were driving down the narrow track that passed for a road, a road that was more or less maintained, mainly less. They were headed for an area that Stream called "the way out there."

Given the usual condition of the road it would be a rather casual drive.

Lou remembered their last trip way out there. It would take three days or so just to get to the first town.

Late in the afternoon, Stream slowed up from a not very fast miles per hour, controlled by the state of the road, the road being what it was, dirt, more or less paved, mostly less, and drove out into the totally barren looking openness, parked, and shut off the truck.

She jumped down and told him as he walked around to join him, "We could camp on the road for as little traffic as there is out here, but one never knows, someone might decided to take a drive at night."

He nodded.

She seemed to need to say that every time.

Walking to the rear of the truck, Stream lowered the tail gate, and began to haul out stuff.

As she began to unfold and set up the table and chairs, she looked at Lou. "I don't think that we will require the tent. I just brought in case. I will make dinner and we can enjoy the open silence out here while we eat."

Stream made dinner and served. It was, for their usual camping style, rather elegant, sitting at a table in chairs, having dinner and then dessert.

As they were not in a rush they had planned to camp by mid-afternoon, play some cribbage, and relax a whole bunch. On the first day they did just that.

With one exception.

After dinner, Stream began to review everything that Cohan had given them.

"Lots of maps," she stated. "Lots of accurate maps, this time. And names."

She looked up.

"There are going to be some very surprised guys."

Finally they checked where the sun was in relation to the far horizon and decided that they could get a couple games of cribbage in.

Having lost both games, again, Lou began to make dinner preparations while Stream yanked out sleeping bags, mats, and pillows from the truck and set up their sleeping space. Then she opened a bottle of red wine and set it on the table "to breathe."

He served the dinner.

"Definitely luxury camping," he stated as he finished the salad and the last roll.

"Um huh," she agreed.

Stream poured the last of the red wine into his

glass, then clinked her glass against his.

"Hope you don't mind a little company?"

Lou checked all around their spot. It was open space as far as the eye could see in all directions.

Stream laughed.

"Before we get to civilization, such as it is out here, in about three, maybe more, days, I expect that we will have some company."

"Oh."

He set to washing what needed washing, dried them, and put the pots and pants, dishes, etc., back in the appropriate boxes and latched the tops.

They sat in the evening, shifting from dim to dark, and listened to the sound of silence.

As the moon eased its way into the night sky they crawled into their sleeping bags.

Lou set his gun in the right spot. And fell asleep.

The sun woke them.

Lou started the coffee pot to bubbling and then started on the rest of breakfast.

They sat and ate and watched the open space begin to glow as the sun rose and touched everything with golden light.

As she crunched on the last piece of toast, Stream nodded at him, and mumbled crumbs.

"We'll just dawdle down the road and camp at mid-afternoon, more or less. I told Rona that we would be there in about four or five days, probably more."

Lou nodded back.

"Sure."

"We'll spend some time with Round Tom first and discuss things."

"Uh huh."

Lou began to wash stuff, dry it, and pack up the kitchen.

Stream rolled up mats, sleeping bags, put everything back into the correct boxes in the back of the truck.

And then, in a no rush sort of a way, they were jolting down the road, insulated container filled with coffee nestled in the spot between the front seats.

At noon, more or less, they pulled off the road and ate sandwiches while sitting on the tail gate.

"This could get messy." Stream sighed.

Lou nodded.

"I don't think, given who these guys are and what they believe in, that they will come along easy."

Lou shrugged.

"I suppose." *He didn't really care whether they did or not.*

He made another sandwich and munched quietly.

He had brought along his "hand cannon." He shrugged. *Some folk's behavior meant that they probably wouldn't live very long anyway.*

He swallowed the last bit, helped pack what little required packing, and they headed on.

They stopped, as planned, in mid-afternoon,

played a couple games of cribbage, each won one game, loafed, ate dinner, relaxed, and slept.

The next few days followed the same routine.

After dinner, Stream clear her throat loudly.

"What?" Lou sat up straighter.

"Once it gets dark, we are going to have some company."

"Oh?"

"Yep."

"Um huh."

"Just some help that we will be getting."

"Nothing to worry about, right?"

"Yep."

Stream opened the folder that contained the maps made by Cohan.

"We are not all that far, sorta, from where the children are being held. After we leave Round Tom's place and get to Rona's we'll get some more help there."

He filled her glass then his.

"It's a good red," he suggested.

She tapped his glass with her's.

"Yep."

They got in one game of cribbage, Lou won. Then they had dinner, and sat and listened to the soft sound of the open space and darkness.

As the moon coasted into the night sky she reached over and tapped his hand.

"Company coming."

Lou looked around.

"Pretty quiet folk."

Stream laughed.

They flowed out the dark and settled around Stream and Lou.

One walked over and sat next to Stream.

"You remember Moon Shadow," Stream asked.

"Sure." Lou leaned forward and said, "Hi, there."

He looked at Stream.

"Seems like a large group."

"She brought three different packs. They are unhappy. She told them that some people were stealing other people's pups."

"They're helping us?"

"Yep. We are going to be doing things at night. They can see, hear, and smell many times better than people can."

"Mexican wolves, right?"

"Yep."

"We didn't bring along any dog food."

Stream smiled.

"No need."

"Spose not." He looked at the wolves sitting and lying all around them. "They gonna visit Rona also?"

"Nope."

Stream stood and wandered out into the packs. She sat in their midst accompanied by Moon Shadow.

Well, he thought, *it appears that Stream might be of a mind to take no prisoners.*

Caretaker

He was the oldest of the group.

The house had been long ago abandoned, abandoned all those many years ago after his wife died.

Then, after the great discovery and the gathering together of those who truly believed, the house had been reclaimed and restored to livability.

Plans had been made.

Plans were in place.

Plans were in action.

The acquisition of the young boys were assigned to the youngest and most able of those who believed.

His job was to insure that those taken were well fed and housed until the necessary number had been gathered in.

Once that was achieved, all would gather in the ancient structure and the great call into the past would bring a new power into existence, a new power for them all.

As he worked in the kitchen preparing an evening meal, he watched the long shadows march across the open space as the sun began its descent into night.

In that gathering dusk he saw a coyote race past, not trotting but running hard, tail streaming behind.

He shook his head, wondering what had spooked that one, set the table and called the boys to come and eat.

The boys had stopped asking questions or talking to him. He didn't care. They had quickly realized that all around the house was just a vast open space with nowhere to run to, nowhere to escape from him or this house

As he cleared the table, one of the group's members arrived and brought into the house another young boy.

The two men talked softly and then the younger left.

He nodded to himself. Soon this part of the great plan would be done.

He cleared the table and began washing the cooking pots and pans, dishes, cups, knives and forks.

He poured the last cup of coffee and sat at the clean and empty table.

He sipped and wondered why it was taking as long as it was taking. But then, they had planned for years so maybe a small amount of time was not really significant.

Soon he would go to bed, the children did this before he did. So, he would check, count heads, and then go to bed himself.

First Strike

The sun was up.

The camp routine was the usual activity.

It was all involved with making breakfast, eating breakfast, cleaning up, and packing things away.

As Lou heaved the last of the camping gear into the back of the truck, Stream walked off and around a small clump of brush.

Lou stood and stared down the road, the dusty track that passed for a road. As far as he could see there was nothing in sight.

"One more camp," stated Stream as she strolled up to him. "Then the next day we will talk with Rona."

"Sure," replied Lou climbing up into the truck. They had already spent a day visiting with Round Tom and Maize.

Stream clambered up and headed them down the track. As per usual, given the condition of this sorta remnant road, it was a rather slow drive, not too slow, not too fast.

As they drove along there was plenty of time to look at the surrounding landscape and talk about this and that.

And eventually, as it always did, lunch time arrived.

They made sandwiches and once again sat on the tail gate and munched away, taking a sip of something cold from one of the coolers.

After each had consumed two sandwiches, what little that required putting away was put away.

And down the road they went once again.

The sun was heading below the far horizon when Stream pulled off the road and parked some distance from the edge of the road.

They quickly set up camp. She cooked and set out dinner. Then they sat and ate it, sipping a nice red wine, enjoying the luxury of truck camping at its most decadent.

Stream leaned back in her chair, took another sip, and pointed.

"What?"

"Look very closely. There is a rather random distribution of houses down that stem road just way over there."

"Our destination?" He stared at it.

Seemed like the right place, all right.

"Yep. We'll drive down there in the morning."

She grinned at him. "It won't be a surprise. I am sure that they already know that we are here. That bunch is very in tune with their environment."

"O.K. We have time for a game or two, depending upon the light," suggested Lou.

They played a game of cribbage, then it was too dark for another. Lou won.

They could have turned on a lantern or two, but didn't.

It was just a very pleasant thing to do, to sit in the dark, to talk, and to finish off the open bottle of red wine.

They laid on their sleeping bags and thick mats and watched the display over head, more stars than anyone ever saw living in a town or city.

In the early morning light of the first rays of a rising sun, Stream waggled one hand at Lou, careful not to slosh coffee everywhere. She had stopped Lou from any further breakfast preparations.

"Leave all that stuff in the truck, we will eat breakfast in a little while."

Lou nodded, rolled up his sleeping bag and mat, and stuck it in the proper box and did the same thing with the rest of their gear, and the table and chairs they had unloaded.

Stream drove them slowly along the road and then turned down the side road toward the scattered dwellings.

Lou looked at the place as they drove along.

Obviously there was no town planner here. The houses appeared to have been placed where ever the owner had felt was the right spot. And everyone seemed to have their own idea of what sort of architecture was to be followed.

Stream turned and parked alongside a large truck that appeared to have never been washed.

"Here we are," she announced as she jumped down and headed for the front door of the house.

As soon as Lou joined her she knocked loudly on the door, opened it, and stepped inside.

A very large man rose from his chair, a large gun on a holster on his right hip and looked at them.

"Stream," he said.

"Rona," she replied.

She turned and smiled at the tall woman who had stepped from what appeared to Lou to be the kitchen.

"Stream," she said.

"Slim Jem," said Stream, smiling happily. "You making breakfast?"

"Just started. It is a special breakfast. You can talk with Rona while I finish." She ducked back into the kitchen.

Stream sat in one of the straight-backed wooden chairs and smiled at Lou as he did the same thing. "You are in for a real treat," she told him.

Rona nodded. And waited. He knew that Stream would get around to whatever had brought her way out here to his town. He felt that it was his town, him being the Sheriff and, essentially, the only law there was.

He looked at Lou. "Let me see your gun."

Stream frowned at Rona.

Lou pushed his jacket aside and slowly removed the gun and made it safe to handle. He offered it to Rona.

"You ever shoot anyone?" asked Rona.

"Sure."

Stream's frown darkened. She knew that Lou could take his gun back any time that he wished, if Rona decided to keep it. She wondered what was bothering Rona. His behavior was unusual, not the same as before. But, as usual, Lou looked perfectly relaxed.

Rona handed Lou his gun and looked at Stream.

"I suppose Lou," he said, "has a permit, etc., for that cannon?"

"Right!" snapped Stream.

Lou reloaded his weapon and put it back in its holster.

He nodded and looked at Rona. "Want to see it?"

Rona shrugged.

Lou unzipped a side pocket, and pulled out a small, dark brown leather case and handed it to Rona.

Rona opened it, eyes scanning whatever it said, his eyebrows jumped up, then he looked from Lou to Stream and back again, snapped the case shut and handed it back to Lou.

Lou set it back in his side pocket and looked back at Rona.

Well, surprise, surprise, big guy.

Rona sat back in his chair and looked at her.

"Stream, you are always a surprise."

Stream looked at Lou.

He shrugged.

She could look at those credentials some time later.

Slim Jem walked from the kitchen and quickly set four places on the table, thick ceramic white plates and mugs, and dropped a handful of knives and forks.

"Push up! Breakfast is ready."

She walked back to the kitchen and returned with two thick white platters, one heaped with large diameter pancakes, the other loaded with fried sausages. Then she returned and brought back a large coffee pot and set it on a hot plate, and sat in one of the chairs.

"Don't wait, take something," she ordered.

Stream was already doing that, so was Rona.

Lou decided that the comment was directed at him, so he did, take something. As he chewed his first bite, he was delighted and surprised. Slim Jem would have to be one of the best chefs in existence. What she had served would be first class in any of the top restaurants anywhere.

Rona took a swallow from his coffee mug and nodded at Lou.

"Folk hereabouts deem it a great privilege if Slim Jem invites them over for special breakfast."

Slim Jem winked at Rona who quickly snatched this third helping of pancakes from the platter.

When all were finally finished, Slim Jem quickly carried everything back to the kitchen, lightly touching Rona on the shoulder as she passed by. She returned and sat in her chair.

Rona leaned back in his chair, front legs off the floor, coffee mug in hand.

"O.K., Stream, what is it?"

"I need some help that I can count on to do exactly what I say."

"For?"

She opened the folder she had carried in and set on the table. It had a large oval stain on it. Slim Jem had set the platter of sausage on top of it.

Sliding out one page, Stream slid it over to Rona.

"This is a map that shows where the captive children are being kept. I am going to release them and see that anyone there goes to jail. But I need some help, some good help."

Slim Jem gasped and looked at Rona.

"And?" prompted Rona as he gently leaned forward, setting the front legs of his chair back on the floor.

"I want four people with long rifles plus you. Those four have to be totally reliable and very, very good shots. At night!"

Slim Jem looked back at Rona.

"Charlie Chews A Lot," she stated. "Wide Annie, Henry, and Old Snap."

Rona nodded.

"Henry is my part-time deputy," Rona told Stream. "He can handle Old Snap. Wide Annie and Charlie will work with me."

"Recognize where this place is?" Stream tapped a spot on the map.

"Aiya! It is due north of here. Long ago abandoned. Bad road that away, mostly overgrown or blown out."

"How close can we get with trucks without causing alarm?"

Rona stared somewhere and then looked at her. "Two washes, two trucks. We can drive, essentially below grade, and park about a mile back some or so. Then we will walk from there."

Stream nodded.

Stream drew a circle around that spot with a pen.

"I want you and you folk to stay way out from the house like this. Nobody shoots anything, not one time. No potshots at wild life running past. If any of your folk can't agree to that, they just stay home. No argument! We need a loose circle around that place. If someone tries to run past, knock them down. If they whip out a weapon, shoot them. It would be nice to have someone to jail."

She looked from Slim Jem to Rona.

"But it isn't necessary," she suggested.

Rona nodded and shrugged. "Won't bother anyone from around here."

Stream nodded back.

"Let me emphasize this. Nobody shoots at anything else. No rabbits! No coyotes! No wildlife! No anything! If anyone can't accept that, or you think they can't restrain themselves, they stay home! If anyone does shoot anything other than some person, some adult person running away, they will be in a world of hurt, if they survive!"

Rona stared at her. He slowly nodded. "I will

make sure they understand."

Stream was as serious as he had ever seen her.

Slim Jem stood and poured coffee into their mugs and checked Rona's expression.

Home Again

They waited by the parked trucks until it was 2:00 a.m.

They waited for that time of night when most folk were at their most removed from consciousness.

Rona decided to have the trucks stop even further away than planned from their objective, just to be sure that no-one would hear them. At this spot the arroyo was very deep, a good place to hide their trucks from sight, dark night or not. He had decided that extra caution was called for.

Stream and Lou had ridden in Rona's truck along with Rona, Wide Annie, and Charlie.

Wide Annie sat in the front with Rona. Lou, Stream, and Charlie filled the rear seat.

After they all clambered out, Rona leaned against one arroyo side wall and checked his watch with a red lens flashlight.

As the watch hands crept into place, he said, "Time to go." Far to the other side of their destination the other truck would be doing the same thing.

The small group walked up the arroyo watching where they walked in the faint light of a moon coasting toward the horizon. It was good enough for a careful approach.

Rona hissed softly, they all stopped.

"Just ahead," he said ever so quietly, "to the left, there is a good spot where we can climb out. Slowly."

And soon enough, they all stood on the surface and began to head for their target, softly, slowly, following Rona.

Finally, Rona held up one hand and pointed.

He, Charlie, and Wide Annie began to spread out while Stream and Lou headed in the direction Rona had indicated.

And, soon enough, Stream and Lou could see the dark shape of a house. Not a light shone through any of the windows.

Stream headed around one side with Lou following, watching everything that he could see.

They stopped by an outside door. Stream leaned close and spoke in Lou's ear. "Watch the door. I'll be back in a bit." She turned and walked away, not making a sound. He could just see her when she had sat down. He could just see the vague shadows gather and settle around her.

He waited.

And waited.

Forms and soft footsteps approached.

They stopped.

"Moon Shadow and two brothers are coming in with us. They understand."

She bumped him gently with a shoulder. "Time to visit."

Lou nodded and carefully eased the door open with one hand, gun held in the other. He was surprised that it was unlocked.

When it was wide open he slithered inside in a low crouch and held it open. Stream and her three shadows slipped into the room. She clicked on her flashlight and aimed the soft red light around the room, the kitchen, and settled it on the doorway opposite the outside entrance.

Moon Shadow and her brothers headed that way. Lou winced at the noise of sharp toe nails clicking on the hard wood floor.

He followed them into the living room, red light shining to one side.

The three wolves stood and stared at a closed door.

Lou nodded and stepped to one side of the door, waved Stream to the other side, not in front of the door. He didn't want anyone standing in front of the door when he shoved it open. If someone inside had a gun and started shooting, they would be probably aiming at where they thought a person would be, not closer to the floor where the wolves were.

Stream nodded, clicked off her flashlight as Lou shoved the door open. The wolves hurtled inside the dark room.

A single voice from inside screamed in terror.

"Bingo!" snapped Stream.

Lou slipped inside, found the light switch, and switched it on.

An elderly male, eyes wide and staring, was in the bed, covers tossed here and there. He had three wolves for company.

Each of his wrists were held in the tightly clamped jaws of a wolf. Moon Shadow stood, paws on his chest, staring down into his face, lips curled back from her teeth.

Stream stepped to one side of the bed and looked down at him.

"I wouldn't struggle if I was you!"

She yanked his ankles together and fastened them together with a plastic tie. Then she eased one wrist from a wolf mouth, yanked it up and tied it to the ornate iron headboard, then the other wrist. Yanking a roll of grey duct tape from her small pack, she tore off a strip and fastened it over his mouth. She didn't want him to try and get at some deadly device in order to escape justice.

"We'll talk later," she told him.

She hurried from the room and into the other bedroom, snapped on the light and smiled at all the suddenly open and staring eyes.

"Heya! You guys ready to go home?"

As the children nodded, frowned, and finally smiled, she added, "Well then, get your stuff packed and be ready to leave this place. Quickly please."

As the children began to do that, she walked back into the living room and snapped on the lights, then those in the kitchen.

And soon she could hear the sound of heavy feet pounding toward the house.

As the rest of her party gathered in the living

room, the three wolves walked from the bedroom and slipped to the outside through the open back door.

Eyes jumped from Stream to Rona and back again.

"Calm down!" demanded Stream. "Everybody just calm down."

Slowly they did.

Then, after some conversation it was decided.

Wide Annie and Charlie would remain in the house and catch alive, if possible, any others that might turn up, especially if they brought other children. The rest would head to their trucks and back to town.

Rona carefully searched their prisoner, searching for anything he thought this guy might think of swallowing. He wasn't interested in watching another of them commit suicide.

Finally satisfied, he cut the man's wrist ties, rolled him over and retied his arms behind his back.

Rona turned and nodded at Stream.

"I'll just tote him back to our truck. He doesn't look all that heavy." He picked the man up and tossed him over one shoulder, saying, "You start squirming or doing anything, I'll just punch your lights out!" He headed for the outside door. "Let's go, Stream."

Stream and Lou helped the children gather up their belongings and led them out the back door.

Stream began to herd the children along, following Rona.

Far to the sides, she could the dark shadows of wolves walking parallel to them. Lou looked where she had looked and wondered where the rest of them had gone.

Stream and children walked along in a cloud of chatter and questions. She kept reassuring them that, yes, they were going home, and yes, that they were safe. The children didn't notice their four legged company.

Their minds were focused on the idea of going home.

Soft Ending

Stream and Lou wound up another weeks work, handed over the final draft to the folk that would make the final product in whatever quantities had been selected prior to delivery to the appropriate agency, doing both the boxing and shipping, etc.

Stream swivelled her chair around and grabbed her phone as it started blinking, listened, and smiled. "Heya, Matias." She nodded to herself. "Sure."

In a moment their office door opened and he walked in.

Stream looked at them, quite a contrast.

Lou wore his usual soft, relaxed attire, which sorta matched his usual appearance, when sitting or standing.

Matias was wearing one of his inexpensive dark suits. Of course, to Matias, "inexpensive" was the equivalent to Stream's weekly salary. Matias' family was what those who had lots of money called "Old Money." He didn't really think about it and never tried to impress anyone with that fact. He felt that what was important was how well he did his job as a detective in the city system.

"Care for an early dinner?" he asked them.

"Sure," replied Stream.

Lou nodded and stood, and fetched his coat.

Matias named the restaurant and headed out the door, saying over his shoulder, "See you there."

Stream laughed. Matias had an aversion to riding in her seldom washed truck.

Stream and Lou headed down the corridor to where she usually parked.

Stream drove across town and finally pulled into a gently curving driveway, and parked under a large covered space in front of the ornate wooden door. She jumped down, leaving the truck running and walked to the door.

Stream looked at Lou, "I decided that we wouldn't go around and do in all those guys on Cohan's list. Other folk can take care of that problem."

O.K."

That is one great problem taken care of.

Lou joined her and watched as a tall man dressed in a well-cut brown suit walked over and gave Stream a ticket, then drove her rig around a far corner of the building.

"Inside," she said, holding the door open.

The stepped into and walked down a short hall to stop at another tall man dressed in a well-cut brown suit.

All the staff at this restaurant were selected and attired in a manner than was a very, very long tradition, dating back before more recent rules began to apply to establishments like this one.

The man smiled at Stream. "Good afternoon, Miss Jansen." He waved a languid hand. "This way, please. The Matias table is just this way."

Lou looked the question at her as they followed along.

She grinned at him. "My father, the Viking! Remember?"

Lou nodded and looked at their surroundings as they tred on a thick carpet to a table set in a secluded alcove. Matias already sat there, on opened bottle of wine in the middle of the table.

It was a very quiet place in spite of the number of patrons.

"This is a very good red," said Matias as he filled three glasses. He lifted one. "Chin chin." And took a sip. Then he smiled at them.

"I thought that we could talk before the food arrives." He laughed softly. "Of course it won't arrive until we are ready for it."

"Ummmm," said Stream as she sat and sampled the wine.

Matias smiled at her. And winked.

As soon as Lou sat and took a sip, Matias cleared his throat.

"All those children are at their homes and seem to be doing all right. Some talented folk will be watching them just to make sure. No one will ever know about them or where they have been." He shrugged. "Just a precaution, that's all."

He looked at Lou. "I am just a city cop with a limited jurisdiction. Umm, we did send copies of Cohan's stuff, thanks to Stream, and with Cohan's permission, to the appropriate folk out there. It appears that many of that nasty group seem to have disappeared in some manner or other."

Matias refilled their glasses.

He nodded at Stream. "Your, ah, captive did tell us quite a bit about their group, ahhh, after we agreed to move him to another part of the country and set him up. Some help from our federal friends. From what he said, it appears that group felt that they could bring someone, something, from another world to this one. It had to do with their mythology. This being would then help the group with their magic. The kids were the main ingredient that would have been used to make this happen."

Lou took a big swallow from his glass. "So that plan is out of action?"

"Indeed it is."

Matias emptied his glass.

A waiter appeared, took the empty bottle, left another in its place, already opened, and disappeared.

Matias looked at Stream

"What?" she asked.

"In the Way Out There," he said.

"Ummm."

"Some of the group did turn up dead, rather badly dead, if one could say such a thing. Mauled by wild animals."

Stream shrugged.

"There was also a rather large, rather strange explosion as well. This one caused quite some excitement among the archaeology folk."

"Oh?"

Matias nodded slowly.

"From what I was told this explosion blew the lid, a wooden structure of some kind, off a site that no-one knew was out there. They surmised this from the rather large circle of debris around the site. There might have been some people in there but it is going take the forensic investigators some time to figure that out."

Stream nodded and shrugged again.

"Good to know," she said, "that group of plotters and planners are out of business. Should be lots of people who are relieved."

Matias nodded his agreement and held up one finger.

The food began to arrive.

"My treat," he said.

"Nice to own a restaurant," she observed.

Lou nodded.

Matias smiled.

As they walked from the restaurant and stood waiting for the valet to bring around Stream's truck, Stream looked at Lou and stated, "I think that you ought to move all your belongs into my house."

She watched him for some kind of reaction.

Lou nodded.

"Sure."

Well, this ought to be interesting.

About the Author

George R. Mead began to study anthropology in 1962 after being discharged (honorably) from the U. S. Army, Combat Engineers. He eventually received a B.A., M. A., and Ph. D. in his chosen field, before that an A.A. in Engineering. Many years later an M. S. W. in Clinical Social Work. He has worked in aerospace, taught at the college and university levels, worked in a community action agency, ran a restaurant, been unemployed, and worked for the U. S. Forest Service. He is now retired from the work-a-day world but does a certain amount of consulting, writing, and research. He lives seven miles outside of the small town of La Grande, Oregon, with his wife, two cats, and one dog named Jettz (all Lab).

www.ingramcontent.com/pod-product-compliance
Lightning Source LLC
Chambersburg PA
CBHW050402030726
47503CB00006B/1975